BEARS OF THE ICE

The Quest of the Cubs

Book 1

KATHRYN LASKY

SCHOLASTIC INC.

The clock did not create an interest in time measurement;
the interest in time measurement led to the invention of the clock.

— David Landes, *Revolution in Time*

THE NUNQUIVIK

Northern Hun[...]
Grounds

Sea of
Nunquivik

Jameso[...]
Ice Fl[...]

Moon
Eyes's Post

To the northern
kingdoms of Ga'Hoole

e Ice Clock

Volcanoes

Ice Spines

g

Oddsvall

Skagen's
Den

THE ICE
CLOCK

Winston

Taaka's
Den

Prologue

The bears' shadows slid across the snow, gobbling the jumble ice that had piled around the den. They were ragged-looking creatures, and *huge*. Across their broad chests were stripes of dark blood. Old blood, not from their own bodies. Most likely from a seal. The realization sent a strange chill through Svenna. Honorable bears did not celebrate the killing of prey. It was one of the first lessons cubs learned out on the ice. The relationship between predator and prey was sacred. One killed for hunger, nothing more. And here these two ragged bears were, strutting about, parading their slaughter.

"What do you want?" Svenna called as the two bears approached. She stepped forward to put herself between the strangers and the entrance to her den.

"We've come for your cubs, madam," said one whose face was crisscrossed with fighting scars.

Svenna's chest seemed to cave into her body, as if she were shrinking in her own pelt. *No.* The word tore through her. *Never.* Svenna had heard terrible rumors about cubnappings, that bears called Roguers were snatching cubs and killing mothers who resisted. That's why she'd left her home and traveled to this harsh land. But evidently, she hadn't gone far enough. The guard hairs on her neck rose and stood rigid. Her claws dug into the snow crust.

"You're not taking my cubs," Svenna growled.

The other one, who was only slightly smaller, replied with a smirk, "It's an honor."

"What's an honor?"

"To give your cubs to the Timekeepers."

"What authority?"

"The Timekeepers of the Ice Cap."

"Never!" Svenna felt a sudden flash of anger and rose onto her hind legs. Her body, which only moments before seemed to shrink, now enlarged, as did her heart, which beat only for her cubs.

"You defy?" The larger bear stepped forward. He smelled foul and had the stench of dead meat, like a scavenger. This fellow did not make clean kills when he hunted. "The penalty for defying the Authority is death, madam."

I can't fight them both off, Svenna thought as panic coursed through her. But she had to do something. "My cubs are not yet named," Svenna said desperately.

"We'll name them."

"*You'll* name them?" she gasped, staggering at the terrible thought. She had to think; think fast. "I'll go! I'll go in their place." The Roguers chuckled, but she continued. "Whatever you need, I'll do it." No matter what, she couldn't let these foul creatures take her cubs.

The scarred bear glared at her with disdain. "We require only cubs."

"I was born and reared in Ga'Hoole, so I know how to read and write. I'm sure I can make myself useful."

The Roguers turned their backs on her and began whispering. Did Svenna dare attack the smaller bear's flank? Her killing teeth could tear into that tender flesh. Would that gain her time — time to flee with her cubs? But before she could act, the Roguers turned back to face her.

"The Mystress of the Hands will be pleased with your service," the scarred bear said. "We accept your trade."

Svenna automatically bobbed her head, as this was the proper thing to do. But there was nothing at all proper about any of this. With each passing second, she loathed herself more and more.

"Are you ready, madam? You can deliver your cubs to a neighbor. We shall follow."

She swayed on her legs as something inside her crumbled. "Give me a bit of time, please. So that I might prepare them."

The larger bear grunted what she assumed to be a sound of agreement. "We will return for you on Tuesday."

"What's a Tuesday?" Svenna asked.

They laughed cruelly. "Be ready then, madam," the smaller one said. "And do not try to escape. We will be watching."

Svenna spun around, feeling the huge bears' eyes drilling into her back as she crawled quickly into the den.

She slid down the slope into the area where the cubs lay sleeping. She looked at them: First, a burly little male; and Second, a slightly smaller female. They were curled up around each other, tucked in a dream perhaps. They were so peaceful, so innocent. So oblivious to the terror that flooded through her. So unconscious of the malice that swirled outside. Her only job on earth was to keep these cubs safe and fed so they could grow into powerful bears, the largest predators in this frozen universe of the Nunquivik and the Northern Kingdoms.

The two little ones twitched in their sleep. First's hind feet kicked as if he were dreaming of ruddering through a current. She hoped it was a dream and not a nightmare about drowning, for First wasn't as strong a swimmer as his sister. Second's tiny pink tongue was flicking in and out — maybe Second was caught in a halibut dream!

She pictured the cruel gleam in the Roguers' eyes, and fear began to flood through her like a great rising tide. She clamped her own eyes shut. *No matter where they take me, I must return for my cubs. I will return!*

CHAPTER 1

Ice Lessons

"We wait for the jumble moon, the one that will drive the tide

And the wintry wind, just 'round the bend

That will bring the ice by the bye

The creaks, the groans, and the mumbles

As the ice piles up in jumbles

And beneath those icy crests

Swim seals in blubbery vests

Let my little cubs learn

before the midnight sun burns . . ."

Svenna sang the song as she led the cubs out to the edge of the Nunqua where the sea met the frozen land, where the jumble ice would soon mass. Jumble ice was the sign that true hunting could begin.

There was no time to waste. That terrible thing called a Tuesday was coming. She glanced back at her two cubs as they scrambled over the piles of ice. They were always looking for the perfect ice slide for skeeters, a game her cubs loved to play. But, sadly, there was no time for that anymore. First and Second had to learn all they could from their mum before those dreadful bears came back.

Svenna had arranged to leave her cubs with a distant cousin, Taaka, in exchange for a rare, valuable filing stone Svenna had brought all the way from Ga'Hoole. It was quite useful for keeping claws sharp enough to slice seal blubber, and Taaka had seemed pleased with the offering. But that was no guarantee Taaka would care for the cubs as her own, so it was essential that Svenna teach them to hunt for themselves.

If Svenna's cubs had been born to the south in the Northern Kingdoms of Ga'Hoole, they would have been named three months after their birth. But here in Nunquivik, the custom was different. It was a harsher land. Many cubs died young; therefore they weren't named until their second season on the ice. So for now, Svenna's cubs would continue to be called First and Second, the order of their birth.

The cubs were squealing with delight over a newly discovered ice slide.

"This one's great! Look how it curves!" First called to his sister.

"Yeah, but I can make it even better!" Second said, bounding over to dig into the ice. "I can make it steeper, faster."

And she would, Svenna thought. Her younger cub had an uncanny gift for building with snow and ice. It was as if Second could see exactly how the crystals locked together. She was what some used to call an ice gazer, though Svenna hadn't heard anyone use that term in a very long time.

"You'd better grip a bit with your hind claws. You might crash," First cautioned his sister, sounding wary.

"Nonsense! I know ice."

"I know you know ice, but be careful," Svenna interjected. "Don't be reckless, Second!"

Second scowled at her mother's reprimand. She wasn't reckless. She was *brave*. Like her father, a great hunter. He wouldn't scold her for being daring. He'd trust her!

First had his unique skills as well. There were occasions when Svenna sensed that her firstborn could pick up the scent of other creatures' thoughts. Some called bears with this particular gift riddlers, for they could riddle another creature's mind.

Just the evening before, Svenna and her cubs had spotted a tern high above their den, and First had said, "She won't nest here."

"Now, how would you know that, First?" Svenna had asked.

"I can't explain. She just won't." He'd shrugged his furry shoulders.

"Why?" Second had asked.

"Something bad happened to her here."

"Okay, but *what?*" Second had prodded, growing irritated.

A troubled look had crossed First's face. "I don't know. But look at her flight pattern. She keeps coming back in at the exact same slant. Then she swivels at the last moment, as if she can't bear to come too close." The guard hairs of Svenna's neck had bristled. First's words had left her with an uneasy feeling.

Watching her cubs play, Svenna had a different sickening sensation. She had not yet told them that she was leaving, and that they'd have to stay with their cousin Taaka, whom they had never met.

"I dare you to do a *gludderwump!*" Second shouted as she scampered toward the ice slide. Second was the most competitive little cub imaginable and was always challenging her brother.

"Of course I can do a gludderwump," First replied evenly. "I taught you how to do it. I showed you exactly how to curl so you roll while you slide."

"So what? I do it better. My rolls are perfect. Tuck my knees, tuck my chin, and off I go."

"Who taught you that knee trick, Second? Me!" First said.

Oh great Ursus, Svenna thought sadly. How she would miss their bickering. But when she called to them, her voice was stern. "Come over here right now, cubs. You're both almost yearlings, and there is much to learn." She stopped herself from saying, "Before I leave."

She had considered running off with the cubs, but the Roguers would find her. Taaka had assured her of this when Svenna sneaked off while the cubs were sleeping. Taaka had not seemed surprised at all about the Roguers. "Happens a lot around here," she'd said brusquely. "There's nothing you can do about it. And don't even think of running away."

"The cubs are still young. They couldn't run far."

"Exactly, and the Roguers are very good trackers. You know of course what they'll do if they catch you?"

Svenna had shaken her head.

"They murder you in front of your own cubs and take them anyway."

Svenna shuddered as she recalled those chilling words and tried to focus on watching the cubs play. It was hard to imagine them hunting yet. They were barely a year old, born on the longest night of the year, the night when the first of the Jumble Roarings Ice begin. But they would have to learn to hunt, young as they were. Taaka had three cubs of her own to nurse. She would have no milk for First and Second.

Svenna felt a twinge in her heart. So much to teach them and so little time! She suppressed a sigh and forced herself to concentrate. There was a chance that beyond the jumble ice some seals might be lurking.

"Come, cubs, it's time to go out a bit and try for seals." The cubs abandoned their slide and bounded over to her, following close behind their mum on their short little legs. "Now what do you remember from the lessons last season?" she asked, trying to keep the anxiety out of her voice.

"Be very quiet," First said.

"No talking," Second added.

"No fidgeting," First said, shooting his sister a look. He knew this would be hard for her. She was so excited. He was too, but he prided himself on being able to hold it back better. Second was not a hold-back kind of cub. "Impulsive," their mum often called her.

The cubs followed their mum, scrambling over the jagged ridge of jumble ice out onto the new ice that stretched before them. It was flat and flawless. This was not the vast Frozen Sea but a bay, and Svenna knew that bays froze sooner. If they were lucky, seals would be swimming below, and her cubs could get some much-needed practice.

"Cubs, look ahead for a shadowy spot in the ice. That's a sign of a breathing hole."

First and Second opened their eyes wide and scanned the ice. Each wanted to be the first to spy a hole.

"There's one!" Second shouted, sprinting ahead. She skidded to a stop and looked down. "No," she said with a sigh. "I was so sure it was a breathing hole."

This happened again and again. Each time Second seemed certain, but each time, she was disappointed.

"Don't worry," Svenna said, trying to sound optimistic. "It takes some time and practice." *But we don't have time*, she thought. If the cubs didn't learn how to feed themselves, they'd never survive without her.

It was shortly after Second's fourth false alarm that First thought he spotted one. He wasn't sure, however, and walked ahead quietly so as not to attract attention. He stopped and looked down, feeling a sudden thrill of accomplishment. A seal breathing hole! He'd found one!

First raised his paw and silently beckoned his mother and sister over.

"Darn!" Second muttered under her breath. She'd so wanted to be first.

Svenna glanced at Second as they walked toward First. "Quiet, dear, and don't look grumpy. Your turn will come. Now, do you remember what do to if you catch a seal?"

"Yes," Second said, as if it were the most obvious thing in the world. "Drag and roll!"

"Good cub," Svenna said, pleased.

When they reached the hole, Svenna signaled with one paw. The cubs immediately went flat on the ice downwind from the hole so the seal would not catch their scent. *Good! They remembered*, she thought, relieved.

It wasn't long before a shiny black nose poked up through the hole.

"I got it!" Second shouted, and pounced. She was quick enough to catch the seal by surprise.

"I'll drag!" First bounded toward the seal, which was flopping on the ice.

"Excellent, cubs! Good teamwork!" Svenna called as she stood by ready to roll the seal and slash its neck.

First had just started to drag the seal from the hole when a shadow engulfed the three of them, bringing a foul smell with it. A shiver coursed through Svenna — that smell! It was the odor of a carrion eater. A creature that stalked true hunters and stole their prey.

Before she could warn the cubs, a voice roared, "MINE!" An immense paw swatted Second, sending her flying through the air, then snatched their plump seal. It was a huge bear with a stripe of blood across his chest and shoulders covered with battle scars.

But Second was not fazed. "NO!" she shouted, outraged, as she scrambled to her feet. *She* had pounced on that seal. Her brother had dragged it from the hole. How could this beast take what was theirs? "Give it back! Give it back. It's ours!" She charged, then, leaping high into the air, smacked down on the bear's head.

"Second, stop!" Svenna roared. One swipe of the stranger's paw could split her daughter's skull wide open. "Let go, Second. Let go!"

But Second clung to the bear and, sinking her claws into his head fur, bit his ear. The bear yowled and shook himself so violently that Second fell off and landed with a crack on the ice.

First felt his stomach drop as the enormous bear rose onto his back legs, baring his teeth. "No!" First shouted, sprinting toward his sister, who lay still. "Leave her alone!"

But Svenna was already charging toward the bear, making a fearsome noise First had never heard before. Before she could reach him, the bear lowered himself back onto four legs, snatched the seal, and lumbered away.

"Second, Second . . . are you all right?" First cried as he skidded to a stop next to his sister. Had the horrible bear knocked her senseless? "Say something!" But she merely blinked and stared at him.

Svenna began gently rubbing snow in her cub's face. "Dear Second, how could you do such a foolish thing?"

A fire suddenly kindled in Second's eyes. "I'm not foolish. I'm mad," she said through gritted teeth. First felt relief sweep through him.

Slowly, Second rose to her feet. "Why'd you say I was foolish? It wasn't fair, Mum. That was our seal!"

"Nothing seems to be fair here," Svenna murmured. Who could have ever imagined that a bear would attack a mother and her cubs? Something had changed in their world. A poison had seeped in. *We are in a lawless place,* Svenna thought. A place swept by winds of violence that could destroy them all.

CHAPTER 2

A Star Named Svern

The sun was hovering over the horizon as they trudged back toward their den. The cubs had recovered from the attack, but Svenna couldn't shake her feeling of unease. Bears didn't steal prey. It was part of the strict honor code that all bears adhered to. She'd never witnessed such barbaric behavior in her lifetime, although she had heard of such things happening during the chaos of the last Great Melting—when the sea rose, flooding the land, and the alliance of bear clans collapsed.

"Itchy!" Second said, stopping suddenly to scratch her ear with her hind foot.

"Oh no!" Svenna sighed, pushing aside her thoughts. "Snow lice?" She saw that First was scratching too. "Well, come over here. I'll pick them out."

Downcast, the two cubs trudged over to their mum. They hated having to sit still while she picked out the pesky mites.

"You first, First," Svenna said.

Second tossed her head. "Mum, it sounds so silly to say *you first, First*. When will we get real names?"

"Just a bit longer." Svenna looked down at the lice. "Nasty little beasts," she muttered as she watched half a dozen drop onto the snow and skitter off. The sun had slipped away. The long night was beginning and the first stars were starting to climb up over the icy horizon. They would soon arrange themselves in the beautiful designs that made the darkness come to life.

"Are bears always named for the stars in the Great Bear constellation?" First asked, glancing up at the darkening sky as Svenna raked her claws lightly through the fur on his head. "And is it true that you can find your way by the stars?"

"They can help a bear navigate, yes. There is one called Nevermoves. If you find the Great Bear constellation, the front paw points to the Nevermoves star. That one is very helpful when traveling, for it always shows the way north."

"Where's your star, Mum?" First asked. "Did it slide away?"

"No, no, it's just that with this new moon the Great Bear is in a slightly different place." She pointed up with one claw that had a little wiggling louse on the end. "In the heel of the hind foot. There's my star, Svenna, for which I was named."

"And where's Da's? I want to know all about Da," Second demanded, stomping her small paw.

Svenna sighed inwardly. It was always very difficult for mother bears to explain about absent fathers. Bears were solitary creatures, and this was especially true for male bears. Males and females came together only in the spring months to mate. The males cared nothing about child rearing. Yet they still often bragged about the offspring they had most likely never met.

Svenna took a deep breath. "Your father's name is Svern, like the star in the hind knee near my heel star. You see, we walk together across the sky. Heel follows knee." Svenna could not figure out why Second was interested in her father. It was unnatural. Cubs never knew their fathers. Why would Second concern herself with a bear she had never met, who had never given her milk?

"But you didn't follow him here, Mum," Second said.

"No, I didn't," she replied carefully. "He's off hunting in the far, far north. Beyond the spot where they have the roarings."

"The roarings? What's that?" Second asked eagerly.

"Oh, it's just something males do when they begin the hunting season."

"Only males?" First asked.

"Yes, females don't make such a big fuss. We just go about our business and start hunting."

"What else, Mum?" Second squinted at the star and tried to imagine her father hunting. If her mum and father could walk together in the sky as a heel star and a knee star, then why could they not walk together on land?

"I don't know much else," Svenna said, eager to change the subject.

"Why not?" Second pressed.

"That's just the way it is, Second. It's the custom."

First growled at his sister. "Second, you ask too many questions."

"And you don't ask enough!" Second snapped.

"Fine. I have one now. What's *that* star?"

"Oh, that's Svree," Svenna said. "See how it points north to the Nevermoves star? Your great-great-grandfather was named for that star in the Long Ago. Of course many bears bore the name of Svree. It was one of the most popular bear names of all."

"Tell us a story, Mum, from the Long Ago," First said eagerly.

"Yes!" Second chimed in. "Tell us one of the bear clan stories. Please, Mum!"

"How your father and I loved those stories," Svenna said, hoping that would appease Second. "That's how we met, searching for stories that came from the Den of Forever Frost. We would often meet near there come mating season." She had a far-off look in her eyes.

"Right," Second said, eyes brightening. "The Den of Forever Frost, where the council used to be. And was it Svree who was king?" Those stories seemed as distant as the stars, but when her mum told them, it was as though she brought them to earth.

"No, Svree, your great-great-grandfather was not called king but chieftain. He was a member, a very important member, of the Bear Council in the Ice Star Chamber."

"And why was it called the Ice Star Chamber?" First asked eagerly.

"Well, there are eighteen stars in the Great Bear constellation, and there are eighteen bear clans, or at least once upon a time there were. Back in the Long Ago, each clan sent a bear of great courage and valor to the Ice Star Chamber. Noble bears they were." Svenna herself had grown up hearing these stories, although it'd been years since the last Bear Council. After the Great Melting, there'd been too much fear, too much chaos. The alliance among the clans broke apart, and soon it was every bear for themselves.

"And these bears ruled the sky?" First asked.

"No, First. No living creature rules the sky. These bears sought only to keep peace here on earth. But now" — Svenna sighed wistfully — "that noble world has vanished. No one tells the old stories. They just fade away into a mist — an ancient mist of a time before time."

They returned to the den, and Second promptly collapsed with exhaustion. But First remained standing. Svenna could feel his eyes boring into her. It was as if this little cub was invading her mind and scraping up every morsel of any random thought.

"Mum," he said in a quavering voice.

"What is it, dear?"

"Mum, something's really bothering you. I can tell."

"Just the lice." Svenna pretended to scratch her ear. "They are pesky little creatures."

Second raised her head sleepily. "Mum, that's not it, is it?" She slid her eyes solemnly toward her brother as she rose wearily to her feet.

Svenna sighed deeply. "First is right. There is something troubling me." She could not cry; she simply couldn't. "Cubs, I am going to have to go away for a while."

"Away?" Both cubs gasped. A look of disbelief filled First's eyes where tears were welling. Second appeared almost angry.

"Where are you going? To the Den of Forever Frost?" Second asked. Her tone implied that this was the only excuse she'd accept. *Of course!* Svenna thought. This was perfect. It was a lie, but sometimes lies were useful. If her cubs thought that she was traveling to a place of legend, of honor and nobility, perhaps it would be enough to sustain them. "Yes, dear, uh . . . there is talk that the Ice Star Chamber is being restored." Hadn't Svern often spoken of this wistfully? It was the single most important idea that she and Svern shared. They'd both believed that unifying the clans and reforming the council was the only way to keep the world of the bears from falling into ruin.

First looked at her questioningly. His nostrils began to quiver. "Mum, do you really have to go?" She could still feel his eyes boring into her, as if he was invading her mind and scraping up every morsel of thought.

"I'm afraid I do, First." She looked away from her elder cub.

"The Den of Forever Frost. Oh, Mum, how exciting," Second said, her face brightening.

Svenna resumed picking out the lice and dared not lift her eyes. She knew First was still watching her. Could he smell lies?

"But what about us?" First asked.

"You'll be going to my cousin Taaka."

"Taaka?" First repeated, trembling slightly. There was no avoiding her elder cub's gaze.

"Who's Taaka?" Second said. "We don't even know her. Why can't we go with you?"

"It's a long, long journey. You're too young. But don't worry," Svenna said quickly. "I'll be back before you know it."

CHAPTER 3

Not Mum

"Hello, Taaka? Here we are," Svenna called down the opening that led into a steep tunnel in the coastal snowbank.

"Oh, come in, come in," Taaka's voice echoed. The cubs scrambled in ahead of their mum. It was a bit of a squeeze.

Taaka was nursing two of her own cubs. "Well, my, my, aren't you big cubbies?" she said sweetly as she looked from First to Second. But First sniffed something beneath the sweetness of her voice and the sweetness of the milk. Something he didn't like at all. "Come right in, little ones. I might have a bit of halibut for you. You like halibut?"

"We love halibut," Second yipped. Clearly, she hadn't noticed anything off about Taaka. First glared at her, but Second didn't notice.

"Well, I'll try and find those scraps later."

"How nice of you, Taaka," Svenna said. "So generous."

" 'Tis indeed generous, I agree. Our stores are paltry. I won't be able to hunt now, you realize, not until these cubs grow bigger." She looked down at her own two cubs. There was a third that appeared to have been flung to the side carelessly. The tiny thing was curled up near her feet mewling. A dark shadow of doubt stole across Svenna's heart. Was this the right bear to take care of her cubs? But who else was there? She was so newly arrived. She didn't know the ways of the Nunquivik.

"Yes, of course. I understand with three cubs, feeding is a challenge." Svenna's eyes rested on the third cub. Birthing three was somewhat unusual. She doubted this one would last. "So, as promised, I brought you this filing stone as a token of my appreciation for taking in my cubs."

Taaka looked at it and sniffed rather dismissively, as if to say, *I've seen better.* But she took it nonetheless.

Svenna felt a tingle of dread. She swallowed and tried to conceal her fear but couldn't dispel the ache of a sob building deep inside her. She turned to First and Second.

"Now, cubs," Svenna said in the calmest voice she could muster. "I know you are going to be good little bears. Mind your cousin Taaka, as it is so nice of her to take you in."

"Mum, are you really going?" Second asked. It was finally sinking in that her mother was leaving, leaving on a great adventure that was excluding her.

"Yes, Second, but it's . . . it's not forever."

"But Da was forever," Second whispered. A few tears escaped from Second's eyes. First had never seen his sister so sad. There was a spark in Second that was as much a part of her as her fur. And now it was dimming before First's eyes. He reached out and put his paw on his sister's shoulder.

"Come outside and I'll give you a hug," Svenna said, her heart breaking.

"Nothing to worry about, cousin," Taaka said sweetly. "We're all family — *clannisch!*"

The cubs followed Svenna out and immediately flung their front legs around her knees. Her fur muffled their sobs as they inhaled deeply, drinking in the scent of their mother, the smell of milk, of blubber, and of stories. After a long moment, Svenna peeled the cubs from her knees.

"Now, now, cubs." She stroked the tops of their heads. "I won't be long. I promise. I'll be back just as soon as I can."

"Promise, Mum?" First asked.

"Of course, dear. I promise with all my heart."

Svenna turned; then, looking back over her shoulder, she waved good-bye and lumbered off. She felt the cubs' watching eyes. Her tears froze on the guard hairs of her face. The cubs waved and waved and waved until she disappeared into the thickening mist rolling in from the sea.

As they crawled back into the den, Cousin Taaka peered at them with narrowed eyes. Something about her had changed in the brief time they had been outside. Taaka was still nursing two of her cubs, who looked plump and fluffy in comparison to the third one, who'd barely moved since they'd arrived. Outside, a bitter wind slashed as a blizzard rolled in. First and Second huddled close to each other, each thinking how on nights like this they would burrow into the soft fur of their mother's thighs. The scent of Taaka's milk stirred the air and made them hungry.

Second squared her shoulders and took a bold step toward Taaka. First was relieved to see that her old spark was back. "About the halibut?" Second said.

"What about it?" Taaka snapped.

"You said you had some. May we have it, please?"

"Oh, that," Taaka replied dismissively. "I've decided I had better save it. This chubby cubby here is growing so fast, he's going to want more than my boring old milk very soon." She cooed at the cub and stroked him gently.

"But . . . ," Second began. First nudged his sister before she could say any more.

"But what?" Taaka made a low growling sound. "You haven't been named, I assume?"

First felt a twinge of fear. It was as if a different bear had taken Taaka's place. The warm twinkle that had been in her eyes when they arrived had dimmed, leaving them dull and unreadable.

First inched toward the edge of the den and peeked out the cave entry to see if their mum was anywhere near. But the blinding storm had swallowed her instantly.

With a sigh, First turned back to Taaka. "I'm First," he said slowly. "And this is my sister, Second."

"That won't do," Taaka snapped.

"Why?" First asked.

"Because *this* is First and *this* is Second." She pointed to the two newborn cubs nursing. "And this one" — she nodded toward the other cub near her feet — "is Third."

Taaka's meaning was clear. First and Second exchanged dismayed looks, and he could tell what she was thinking. *Why should we be Fourth and Fifth? We're older by many moons than these three little lumps.* First had to admit that they *were* rather lumpish-looking. Their eyes had not yet opened.

"Now listen carefully," Taaka barked. "There are the rules here. First of all, there will be no milk for you. I hardly have enough for Third. And he's already giving me trouble. Won't sleep. Has bad dreams or something. Always crying out in his sleep. Little idiot!"

First winced. How could a mum call her cub an idiot?

Taaka removed her own First from her chest and held him up in the air clucking and cooing at him. "This little fellow is a glutton," she said cheerfully. "Were you a glutton, Fourth?" The two cubs blinked. "Well?"

First was confused. *Does she mean me? Am I Fourth now?* "Oh, sorry. I'm not used to being called Fourth."

As she watched, Second felt fury building inside her. Why was her brother apologizing to Taaka? Second was ready to smack her.

"Well, get used to it," Taaka snarled.

"My brother was never a glutton," Second said, raising her chin. "He always shared."

"No back talk!" Taaka growled and showed her fangs. First yelped and scooted back toward Second. Their mother never ever showed her killing teeth, even when she was extremely annoyed with them.

"Fifth is *your* proper name. Now say your brother's proper name. Say it!"

Second felt monumental forces struggling within her. She wanted to lunge at this bear. Rip her nostrils to shreds. But what could she do? Taaka was more than four times her size. Her claws sharpened by the very file their mum had given her. Second was absolutely powerless.

"He's Fourth," she whispered, and felt something shrivel deep within.

"Can't hear you! Again, please!" Taaka raised a paw to her ear as if to hear better.

"Fourth!" Second shouted. But in her head different words rang out. *My brother is First. I am Second. No matter what you*

call me, I am Second! And my brother is First. So there, you . . .
you . . . pile of steaming musk ox scat!

Taaka narrowed her eyes. "That's better." The cub called
Third began whimpering.

"*Urskadamus!*" Taaka muttered, sliding her eyes toward
him in disgust.

"She used a curse word!" First whispered, but not softly
enough.

Taaka's head whipped around. "You'd swear too, you little
fool, if you had given birth to three!"

"Well, that's not really possible, ma'am," Second said. "First
is male."

"Go to sleep right now!" Taaka roared. "That corner over
there. And don't even think about touching the halibut."

"But we're hungry," Second said in a quiet, shaky voice
First didn't recognize.

"No food for rude little cubs."

There was no food that night. Nor the next morning. The
cubs were hungry and they were bored. Taaka never told stories. She never talked to her cubs at all except to say, "Get off,
First, you've had enough." Or "Stop mewling, Third." Yet she
very rarely let Svenna's cubs out of her sight and refused to let
them outside to play. This disturbed First considerably. He
didn't like the way she stared at them, a hungry gleam in her
eyes.

That afternoon, Taaka finally allowed them a small piece of the halibut. It only seemed to make them hungrier, especially once they were forced to watch as Taaka's oldest cub ate his first solid food. It was a large chunk of the halibut.

"You can lick those bones in the corner if there's anything left," Taaka said with a smirk.

Wearily, First and Second rose and began picking over the pile of fish bones in a corner of the den. First uncovered one bone that, although small, was much thicker than that of a fish. As a matter of fact, it didn't have the salty flavor of fish at all.

"What's this?" he asked uneasily, feeling one of the strange sensations that made his mum call him a Riddler.

"Never you mind," Taaka snapped before turning back to her eldest cub. "Oh, you darling little roly-poly thing!" Taaka cooed in delight. "More? You want more?"

"Yes, Mama!"

The cub devoured another chunk.

"Please, Taaka?" First said tentatively. "Could we have a bit more of the halibut?"

"No. I'm saving that for my little Second's first meal." Taaka sighed. "I thought your mother said you knew how to hunt? You've been having a nice comfy time here. Time to get to work. I won't stand for you taking food out of my cubs' mouths just because you're feeling lazy."

"But you wouldn't let us outside," First said.

"Are you back talking me, Fourth?"

"We . . . we can try hunting tomorrow," Second said wearily. "But if we don't eat before then . . ." She trailed off.

Taaka jerked her head to the side. "There are berries over in that corner. I saved them from summer."

The cubs scurried over, but the berries were as hard as pebbles and did little to help the gnawing hunger.

First had begun to grow dizzy and could swear he could feel himself shrinking under his own pelt.

Outside, the storm was still raging. The wind was wild and screeching across the frozen sea. Second glanced at her brother, who was slumped against the wall. There was a dull sheen in his eyes. "First," Second whispered softly. "First!" He didn't seem to hear her. But she could not say his name too loudly or she would be scolded for not calling him Fourth. "Are you all right?"

"I . . . I'm fine. I'm getting used to the hunger."

"No, First, don't get used to it." She nudged him. There was no response. "First, listen to me! We have to get out of here." But the words bounced off him. He did not stir.

Second was growing more and more desperate. Her brother's breath had become uneven. There were longer and longer pauses between each breath. *Is my brother going to die?* Wild gusts of despair were flailing inside of her. She looked over at Taaka, who was cuddling her two biggest cubs. The third one was weakly trying to make its way to her milk. A dark coldness began to invade Second. They had to leave. If she had to haul her brother out of this den herself, she would. She started to prod him.

"Leave me alone, Second," he growled softly. "I just want to sleep." If he slept, he might not wake up. Deep inside, Second knew this would be true.

She nipped him lightly on his haunch. He flinched and gave a little yelp.

"Eating your brother, are you?" Taaka chuckled drowsily.

First stirred. Taaka's words startled him from his thick lethargy. He opened his eyes and stared at Taaka. A terrifying realization took shape within him. That bone! The strange one that wasn't salty, the bone of a smallish creature. A creature not quite grown. It had come from a *cub.*

She's waiting for us to die. Then she'll eat us! First thought, as disgust and horror filled him. There was a peculiar, hungry look in Taaka's eyes. Her tongue slipped from her mouth and licked her lips as if she were already tasting their blood.

In that electrifying moment, Second sensed her brother's alarm and understood what was happening. She felt the cold spike of death in the air.

Wait. Second mouthed the word. First nodded. They would wait until Taaka fell asleep and then they would make their escape. They couldn't risk spending one more night in this terrible place.

They didn't have to wait long. As soon as Taaka's rumbling

snores filled the den, the two cubs climbed noiselessly up the chute, which seemed to have grown in length. They heard Taaka roll over. There was a squeak from her big cub.

"Drat!" she muttered.

First and Second froze. If Taaka woke up and found them halfway up this chute, it'd be over for them. First's heart was thudding so fast in his chest, he was sure Taaka would hear it. They waited. They heard her sigh. Then belch. And then finally snore. First exhaled silently, then signaled Second, and they continued, clawing their way up the last bit and into the maw of the ferocious storm.

In the biting air, each cub let out a long sigh of relief. Better to be devoured by slashing winds and bitter cold than gobbled by Taaka. Then, without another word, they took off, sprinting as quickly as they could. Every force in the universe seemed to fight against them. It was what their mother called a gnaw blizzard, where the very crystals of snow were sharp as teeth and bit through their fur. But they were beyond feeling pain. It was only fear that coursed through them like a mad river. Shoulder to shoulder, leaning against the savage wind, the two cubs attempted to make their way through the storm.

CHAPTER 4

The Grieving Den

The black dome of the sky jittering with stars hung over the vast white world of ice, a world that now seemed too big. Second looked up. Without their mum, the stars were nameless. She could not find the great starry bear, let alone the knee star for which their father had been named. Or the heel star of their mother, or the two little wandering stars, Jytte and Stellan, that their mum said trailed the big bear through the night. Those stars, family stars, were lost.

Second wasn't sure how far they had gone when the two cubs tumbled into a slight depression. She didn't even let out a yelp as she hit the ground. At least they were now protected from the wind.

Second sighed deeply as she settled back against a soft

cushion of snow, then wrinkled her nose. "It smells funny back there," she said, and nodded toward the rear of the wallow they had fallen into.

First sniffed. "What does it smell like?"

"Not Mum," Second sighed. "Do you suppose that we could maybe go find Mum?"

"She's gone to the Den of Forever Frost, the Ice Star Chamber."

Second bristled. "That doesn't mean she's *vanished*. She's out there somewhere."

First was growing agitated. His sister was so impulsive. How could she think that they could simply set out across the Frozen Sea and find their mum! *She never thinks things through.* "Even if we wanted to catch up with her, we don't know which way she went. All the stories she told us about the Den of Forever Frost, she never told us where it was. But none of that matters right now. We have to find some food." His stomach gave a great rumble, as if to emphasize that fact.

Second thought for a moment. "Fine. If you don't think we can find Mum, I have an even better idea."

"What's that?"

"Let's find our father!" Second clapped her paws together.

"Are you completely *kaplunga*? He's already left us once."

Second looked up at the sky, searching for the knee star named for her father, Svern. *No,* she thought. *I am not crazy.*

But First was right. Before they did anything, they had to eat. She turned to her brother. "Fine. Let's go find food. Then we'll decide what to do."

First sighed with great relief. "Now that is truly a sensible idea!" He gave his sister an affectionate cuff.

So the cubs rose up and began once more to stagger along, keeping near the wallow in case they needed to find shelter again. The snow-covered land was sculpted by the wind into snow dunes, occasional hillocks, and mounds, with small winding troughs between them. But this snowscape could change depending on the direction of the wind. It was a constantly shifting maze in which knolls could be flattened or new sharp ridges might emerge.

First paused as he heard a scurrying beneath the snow. "Lemmings?" he said. He had a dim recollection of their mum talking about lemmings. The roundish little rodents were plumper than mice, with beady eyes.

Second nodded eagerly. "How do we get at them?"

"Well, we can't catch them by their tails, as they almost have no tails. Mum told us that. But she said they had some fat."

"You mean blubber."

"No, not that kind of fat. But we can't be picky." Once again First's stomach growled. Hunger was a sharp thing. It cut into you, burrowed into you, making you feel not just weak but light-headed. Right now, all he needed to do was hunt, and to hunt he must think. But he was feeling dizzy from hunger. He lowered his head to the ground and tried to listen.

Second saw a spark appear in her brother's dark eyes. First seemed to regain strength as he grew alert. *He must have heard something*, thought Second, *a skittering beneath the snow's crust.*

She watched as her brother bounded headlong into a drift. There was a soft explosion of snow. First emerged, batting his eyelashes, then sneezed. Two small snow geysers erupted from his nostrils.

"Get any?" Second asked.

"No," he replied glumly. "I could have sworn there were a bunch of them down there."

"Well, I'm not sure if rodent would taste very good."

"I'm so hungry, I'd eat anything right now."

The cubs wandered back across the shifting snowscape of windswept ridges and mounds, growing colder and hungrier with each step. "Maybe we should rest," First said hoarsely as they returned to the wallow. It was a small den compared to those of bears, but it looked as if there were remnants of nesting materials, including clumps of moss and lichen. It looked soft and inviting, good for curling up and taking a quick nap. So, shivering with cold, they curled up together on one of the larger piles.

Sleep came only in short bursts. Each time, the cubs awakened, they felt a terrible sense of loss, though for a brief moment they could not remember why. When they did remember, the pain was even worse.

A figure appeared seemingly from nowhere, and almost indistinguishable from the snow in its whiteness. The cubs blinked. The figure had not entered from the opening the cubs had stumbled through. Two golden eyes gleamed at them. The rest of the creature was the whitest white either of them could imagine.

The creature remained perfectly still except for her delicate ears, which pivoted this way and that, as if trying to pick up something beyond words. *This must be the source of the strange smell*, First thought. He watched carefully. She was smaller than they were, but older. And like the tern he had spotted flying overhead days ago, this creature had lost something dear to her.

Finally, the animal spoke. "What are you doing here?" It dawned on First that this strange little creature, with her sharp tiny face and pointy ears, was a Nunquivik fox.

First and Second exchanged glances. It was the height of rudeness to enter another creature's den without offering a gift.

"I'm sorry. We have no seal scraps," First said, dipping his head slightly.

"Of course you don't. You're not out on the ice yet. You take me for a fool?"

No, First thought. Looking at her, First realized that he would never take this creature for a fool. According to their mum, these foxes were steeped in knowledge of bears, of seal hunting.

"Oh no, never!" First said quickly. "But how did you get in here?"

The fox gave a quick flick of her head. "Another tunnel. Yonder. I knew you were here."

"How?" Second asked, eyes narrowing shrewdly.

"I have ears, don't I?" She twitched her ears this way and that. *Can she sniff with her ears?* First wondered.

"You heard us?" First asked.

"We foxes have the best hearing of any creature in the Nunquivik."

Second was growing nervous. "Do we have to leave? We can't go back to Taaka."

The fox did not reply for a moment. "No, I suppose you can't go back. Taaka's mean as a weasel. And there's nothing meaner than a weasel."

First felt a flood of relief, but not enough to sweep away his uncertainty. This fox could be a friend, but then again, they had nothing to offer her.

"Your mum must have been in a desperate situation if she left you with Taaka. Where did she go?" the fox asked.

"Our mum had to go to the Den of Forever Frost," Second said, a note of pride in her voice.

"The Den of Forever Frost? Is that what she told you?" the

fox asked. A dark shadow clouded her golden eyes, sending a shiver through First.

"Yes," First replied. "Like in all the old stories. Do you know about it?"

"Never heard of the place," the fox said quickly. But there was something behind the golden gleam in her eyes. First had seen the same anxious look in his mum's eyes when he had asked her what was bothering her.

The fox sighed deeply. "Look, this part of the den that you tumbled into happens to be my grieving chamber."

"What's grieving?" First asked, although he sensed it had something to do with loss. The fox clamped her eyes shut briefly, as if she were thinking very complicated thoughts.

"Grief," she said slowly, "is what you are feeling right now about your mum. It's when someone you love is taken from you."

"But she wasn't taken," Second said. "She left us. I don't understand why she would leave us with Taaka. If she really loved us . . ."

"What do you mean *if?*" First cut her off, eyes flashing. "She had no choice, Second. She loves us! How could you think anything else?"

Second knew First was right. Their mum loved them. But how could she have done what she did? How could she have left them with Taaka? It was almost as if another mother, a false mother, had invaded their real mum. Was such a thing possible?

"Are you missing your mum too?" Second asked the fox.

"No, I am missing my kits."

"What happened to them?" Second asked. First tried to give her a kick. His sister could be very nosy.

"Two big snowy owls carried them off."

"That's horrid! Why would an owl do that?" Second asked.

"Why?" the fox repeated. "To eat, of course."

The pain in the fox's eyes was almost unbearable for First. He felt as if he'd been pulled directly into the fox's head. There was a storm of horrifying images as the fox recalled the sight of her kits bleeding and struggling in the talons of the snowy owls, and then watching, helpless, seeing them slowly dissolving into the clouds as the birds flew off.

"I'm sorry," the fox said. Her eyes grew soft. "You don't know about such things. I should have realized that bear cubs are not accustomed to the idea of being eaten. Your kind, after all, are the largest predators on earth. Nothing eats you. You're the top eater, or you will be soon when you're grown-up."

The cubs fell silent for a moment. "I'm . . . I'm so sorry about your kits," First said gently. "What's your name?"

"Lago. And yours?" Her ears made those tiny pivoting motions, as if she could pluck their names right out of thin air.

"I'm First," First said. "And she's Second."

"Our mum used to tell us stories about you," Second said.

"About me?"

"Well, not about you exactly. Make-believe stories about foxes."

"Oh, those silly stories, the Ki-hi-ru stories, about she-foxes turning into musk ox or seals or even bears."

"Yes! There was one about a fox and a bear. But the bear didn't know he had taken a fox as a mate because she had changed her shape into that of a bear, and —"

"Pure nonsense!" Lago chuckled. Her laugh was high and squeaky. But when First looked into her gleaming golden eyes, he saw something lurking behind the mirth.

Fear.

CHAPTER 5

Lago Worries

Lago let the cubs spend the night in her den. She had no food for them, but at least she could provide shelter.

When dawn broke, Lago nosed the cubs awake. "Come with me," she whispered. She had spent enough time in her grieving chamber. She had to get out on the ice if she wanted to grow fat and find a new mate. But first she'd take one last plunge into the snow for a mouse to sustain her on the journey, and find a few for the poor cubs. Maybe she could teach them a thing or two about rodent hunting.

The two cubs crept out onto the snow crust after her. Crouching very low, Lago slithered across the crust, her head wagging ever so slightly this way and that. They watched her ears flick just the tiniest bit. Suddenly the fox leaped straight up into the air, her body suspended in an arc over the snow. Then, headfirst, she dived straight down, plunging deep into the powdery white. When she emerged, she had two mice in her teeth. The cubs were astonished. Was she bird or fox? For indeed in that moment she had seemed to fly.

Lago trotted over to them and dropped the mice at the cubs' feet. "Try them. You probably won't like them. But you have to eat something. And there's more down there."

The mice were plump. Although they found the taste somewhat revolting, the cubs gobbled them up.

"But don't you need them?" Second asked as Lago dropped two more in the snow for them.

"I can make do for now."

"How did you even find them?" First asked. He hadn't heard or seen any sign of the creatures at all.

"I've got — well, all foxes have — the Northing."

"The Northing?" First repeated.

"It's something that we are born with. The Northing helps us find our way no matter where we are. And it helps us hunt. It's like a sparkling line in our head that matches up with a deep line in the earth. We measure all things from it. It becomes a guide for us."

First nodded. "Mum told us about a star called Nevermoves that helps bears when they are out on the sea ice. Is it like that?"

"A bit, perhaps. But not exactly." Lago gave the cubs a look they couldn't quite identify. "Now I must be going. There's a bear I want to follow onto the ice." She tipped her head, as if she wanted to say good-bye but couldn't quite utter the words. Then she turned and trotted off.

The cubs watched her go with a pang. Her shadow sprawled across the moonlit snow and finally disappeared as she headed toward the edge of the Frozen Sea.

Second wheeled around to First and whispered in a strangled voice, "Why couldn't Mum have left us with Lago?"

"She's not our kind," First replied.

Second tipped her head in the direction of Taaka's den. "But did Mum think *she* was our kind?" Her eyes grew fierce as the idea she'd pushed out of her head returned, filling her with warmth. "We don't have a choice, First. We need to find our father." Second knew that once their father laid eyes on his cubs, he'd never abandon them. He'd protect them. He'd love them at first sight.

First sighed. "When will you understand that fathers have nothing to do with their cubs? It's not that they love us or don't love us. They don't know us, and that is the custom. Don't you understand?"

"No! No, I don't," Second exploded. "The word 'custom' has no meaning for me. It's a stupid word. It's just an excuse not to think about anything."

First felt his heart sink. He could see the sob quaking within Second like a wave about to break. "I . . . I . . . didn't mean to make you so upset." He put his front leg around her shoulders. "Second, we can't fight. All we have in this whole wide world right now is each other."

His sister's face crumpled. Tears slid from each eye and were frozen solid by the time they reached the guard hairs of her muzzle.

"You're right," he continued. "We don't know when Mum's coming back, and we'll never make it on our own. We have to try to find our father."

Second stared at him, startled. "Really, First? You want to go find Da?" A current of excitement passed through her, and she began to jump from side to side. "But where do we go? How do we know how to find him?"

First considered this. "Mum said he's hunting in the north."

"But how do we get to the hunting grounds?"

First looked about. The world had turned white, as land and sky merged into a singularity of nothingness. But for the first time, he felt undaunted. "We just have to wait until the storm blows itself out. Until we can see the stars, the one called Nevermoves. Mum said if you follow it, it'll guide you to the north."

And so the cubs, clinging to each other, rolled into a ball, a small bundle against the ferocious wind, and waited for the stars to return.

When their hunger grew too much to bear, they hunted mice. But there was something wrong with the rodent food. It did not satisfy. Within a short time, their stomachs were making angry sounds. Hunger was their constant companion. Just when First was beginning to regret their plan, the storm started to clear and the stars appeared.

"Look!" First shouted. "There it is."

Second wiped her eyes. "It's there. The Nevermoves — right where Mum said it would be, just off the forward paw of the Great Bear. It's waving to us. It's saying, follow me. Follow me! And look, those two little stars, Jytte and Stellan, are skipping ahead, straight for it!"

By the time the storm had blown itself out, the tips of their guard hairs were spangled in icicles and radiant in the light of the stars.

The cubs were shivering—shivering but happy. They staggered to their feet and began to follow the scent of the ocean. They would go out onto that great frozen sea and become real hunters — hunters of seal and not mice! They would grow to be the largest predators on earth. By the time they found their father, they'd be expert hunters, and he'd have no choice but to be proud of them.

They walked through the rest of the night until the first

glimmer of the dawn began to glow on the horizon, swallowing the stars one by one. But they were heading north — to the hunting grounds of their father. Of this they were sure.

And so they continued through the dawn and into the dim light of a new morning. Two little cubs, just tiny specks in the vast white world of Nunquivik, headed toward a boundless frozen sea.

CHAPTER 6

Another Creature's Secret

They had not been long under way when First felt an odd sensation. He stopped in his tracks. The wind had died, and an eerie stillness crept over the landscape. The weak sun appeared rimed with frost. And everything from the sun in the near colorless sky to the ice seemed brittle and on the verge of shattering.

"We shouldn't go this way."

Second spun around. "Why not?"

"It's dangerous. There's something hidden here. I . . . I can't explain it exactly, but I feel it's another creature's secret."

Second sighed. If they had to stop every time First had one of this weird "feelings," they'd never make it to the northern hunting grounds. "What are you talking about, First? Another creature's secret?"

"I smell halibut . . . and seal . . . It's another animal's hoard of food."

Despite the fear in First's voice, Second's mouth began to water. But before she could ask how they might find this food, a creature with spiky black fur exploded from behind a pile of ice.

"Mine!" a voice shrieked.

Something hurled itself against First, who went skidding. For a moment, he couldn't breathe, couldn't even move. *Help!* First tried to shout, but the full weight of the creature was on his windpipe. Just when his vision started to blur, the beast pivoted sharply and ran toward Second, its teeth bared, an evil light flashing in its eyes.

No! The word tore through First as he watched in horror. Wheezing, he scrambled toward his sister, but before he could reach her, the creature grabbed Second and flung her to the ground.

Skunk bear! His mum had told them about these dark, bristly furred animals. They were smaller than bears but incredibly vicious and strong. Their fangs were dreadful, very long in comparison to the short, sharp teeth squeezed in between them. They seemed to have more teeth than their mouths could hold.

Second writhed and gnashed her teeth, but she couldn't shake her attacker loose. Its strength was shocking. *It's crushing me!* Its short, stocky legs were gripping her midsection, and she felt as if every breath of air was being squeezed out of her.

First watched in horror as the creature lifted Second off the ground. It threw back its head, squashing the cub harder and harder. Second was gasping for breath.

He'll break her, break her in two! Desperate, First launched himself into the air from behind the beast, landing on its back. He dug his claws into the skunk bear's skin, holding tight as he could as it thrashed from side to side. With one leg, First reached around and swiped at the creature's face with his claws, tearing the nostrils. There was a terrible snorting sound. Blood spurted into the air.

The skunk bear dropped Second and began howling, blind with fury. In the bloodstained snow were the black fragments of what had been his nose. The sounds that came from him were distorted. His breathing seemed mangled.

First grabbed his sister, and then, half dragging and half carrying Second, bolted. They were some distance away when Second seemed to recover herself.

"I'm all right! I'm all right."

"Did he break anything?"

"No, no." Second looked up at her brother in awe. "You did it, First. You saved my life!"

"I did?" First replied, stunned. It was now all a blur to him. He looked back and, in the distance, could still see the skunk bear convulsing on the ground. "I don't think he'll follow us."

"I don't think he could find us. You wrecked his sense of smell, First. He'll never be able to track us or any other creature again." She looked at him with an expression he'd never seen before. Admiration. "You're powerful, First."

But hungrier than ever, First thought. They had to find food soon.

They continued north, scrambling over ridges of jumble ice, but so far they had not seen the one that ridged the Frozen Sea. Second stopped and lowered her muzzle until it was half buried in the snow. Was she smelling true sea ice? First wondered. Had they come that far? Second started off haltingly in one direction but had gone only a few paces before she turned sharply. She slowed but continued in the new direction, plowing through the snow with her entire muzzle. First recalled his mum's words: *Your sister is an ice gazer.*

"An ice gazer? What does that mean?" First had asked.

"The ice is a mystery. It contains secrets within secrets, and your sister can parse them. Just like your father. He too was a gazer. Both of them can smell the snow, the ice — the rotten ice, the dryness of freshly fallen snow of the First Seal Moon, and how it differs from the Seal Moon that follows."

Second reared up and waved one paw in the air. "We did it. That last ridge from this morning was the rim of the Frozen Sea. This way! This way! I smell the salt and I hear the water far beneath the ice sea."

Both cubs felt a flutter of excitement as they walked on.

This would be their test. Could they do it? Could they find seal on their own? Gradually they began to push out their doubts with a staunchness of spirit and grit. *Heart grit* their mum had called it. Yes, they had heart grit. That was what she told them a bear needed to survive. And so their walk became a march, a march across the ice with Nevermoves as their guide, and in their heads a plainsong thrummed. *No more mice, no more rodents!* They were hunters, hunters of the sea, of the big-blooded animals that would make them fat.

All the while they reviewed the lessons for still-hunting their mum had taught them. Still-hunting, she had told them countless times, was just what it sounded like — being very still. First wondered if Second, with her impulsive nature, could be very still, and if so, for how long?

They walked and walked. They could see the soft glow in the distance where the sun would never really rise but was only a stain on the horizon, a faint shade of red from another world where it was truly morning.

CHAPTER 7

Moon Eyes

The land under their paws felt different. There was none of the eerie stillness that had enveloped them before they encountered the skunk bear. Even the air smelled different here.

A new sound began to thread the air, a sound neither one of the cubs had ever heard.

"What is that?" Second asked, a tremor of excitement in her voice.

"I'm not sure." First angled his head to hear better. It was a distant sound, like a muffled thunder. He could even feel a light vibration beneath his feet. "Second, it's a roaring. It's the sealing season beginning. Remember what Mum said about males roaring and —"

Second's eyes grew bright. "And females stand quietly by! Not me!" Second began to roar, though it was not quite the deep, thunderous sound of the big-chested bears. "If that idiot skunk bear hadn't squished me, I would be able to do this better." She pouted and tried again.

First chuckled to himself. Second was not exactly what one would call humble.

The roaring was thunderous but at the same time jubilant. The clamor grew louder as they drew closer.

"There must be so many bears out there, First! Maybe one of them can help us find our father!"

They sped up, walking steadily in the direction of the roaring. Suddenly, a deep voice split the air.

"Toothwalker out of water on ice approaching roaring. Beware!" The cry raked the night, and the cubs skidded to a halt. "Not you, cubs. Don't worry." The bellow came from a mass of ice slabs that had piled up one atop the other at odd angles a short distance ahead. Sitting on the summit was a bear so still that they had taken him as part of the ice formation.

Second, rarely at a loss for words, now struggled to speak. "Wh-what . . . what are we seeing here?"

"I take your question to indicate that you have seen, but do not comprehend, my peculiar condition," the bear said. There was more silence. "I can hear your breathing but no words come out. I could tell that you're cubs from the strike of your paws against the ice as you ran."

"Can't you see us?" First asked, for the bear was swinging his head about but never settled his gaze upon them.

"Your eyes are blank," Second said. Bears' eyes were dark — a rich, deep brown, almost black — but these eyes were completely white. White as snow, white as ice.

"Not quite true," the bear said. "Once I had eyes. But now the sockets are packed white with *issen blauen*. And so I am called Moon Eyes."

"What is issen blauen?" Second asked.

"It is the highest-quality ice in the world."

"Does it help you see?" For once, First didn't chafe at his sister's nosiness, for he was dying to ask the same questions.

"No, I am still blind, for my eyes are no more."

But *blind* seemed the wrong word in Second's mind. The bear did not seem to need eyes. Second felt as if this bear could see her in a different way, a manner that did not require eyes.

"Why are you sitting here and not at the roaring?" Second asked.

"I am a guard."

First tipped his head to one side. "How can you be a guard, if you cannot see?"

"I can hear. I heard your footfalls, didn't I? I could tell you were cubs. Cubs entering your second year, I believe." The cubs looked at each other in wonder.

"So what do you guard against?" First asked.

"Weak ice, breakthroughs from which toothwalkers might climb. I listen for these perils, and then I roar to signal the other bears to scatter. But I guard not simply against, but also for."

"What does that mean?" First asked.

"I guard for our old way of life — a way of life that is disappearing in the Nunquivik. The noble traditions have been forgotten." He shook his head sadly. "Nothing has been the same since the Roguers arrived in these parts."

"What . . . what do they do?" First asked nervously, not liking the sound of that word.

"They are savage. They seize cubs, for the most part."

"*Seize* cubs? Why?" Second was stunned.

"To take them away to a dangerous place. To enslave them, it is said."

"So how do you know who's a Roguer and who's not?" First asked, glancing over his shoulder at the empty expanse of whiteness they'd just crossed.

The bear Moon Eyes tapped his nose. "I can smell the Roguer because he has the scent of the Ublunkyn. You know what the Ublunkyn is?"

"No, sorry," First said.

"The Ublunkyn is the region of the Ice Cap, far from here, but not far enough. Never far enough. That is where they take the cubs. That is where bears forget the old ways — they forget the ways of hunting, and the traditions of the clan bears. They forget their stories, their history. They forget the ways of Svree."

Despite the sound of the roaring, a pocket of silence seemed to envelop the cubs and the blind bear.

Second leaned in closer to Moon Eyes. "You say you can smell the Roguers because of the smell of the Ublunkyn. So the ice there is different from this ice?"

Moon Eyes's nose quivered. "Yes, the ice is very different there. I'll never forget its scent."

"Why?" First asked.

"That is a long story and a sad story." He sighed. "You see, it was the Roguers who blinded me many years ago when I was just a cub. They tore out my eyes when I dared to run away."

CHAPTER 8

The Story of Moon Eyes

The cubs sat on a slab of ice just beneath Moon Eyes's perch. He looked down at them with his unseeing orbs of white issen blauen.

"When I was a cub, perhaps even younger than you, certainly smaller, I was captured by brutal bears and taken on a long journey. When we finally arrived in the Ublunkyn region I saw a chance to make a break for it. It was the second time I had tried to run away from them, and they decided I was too troublesome and that I would make a better Tick Tock if I were blind. So they tore out my eyes."

Second shuddered with disgust at the terrible image. "A Tick Tock? What is that?"

"I don't know exactly, because I escaped before I got to the Ice Cap."

"And you escaped even though you were blind," First said.

"Yes, finally I did. You see, when they blinded me, I began to bleed heavily. So they packed my empty eye sockets with ice. It was issen blauen, the ice of the Ublunkyn, and it has a very peculiar odor. The scent filled my head and blocked every other scent almost entirely.

"When those Roguers blinded me, they never thought I would dare escape, and they became careless while guarding me. So I did dare. I knew I could smell my way out, for I knew that when the scent of Ublunkyn ice began to fade I would be heading in the right direction — away from the Ice Cap."

Second wondered if she could have gotten away if her eyes had been torn out. Would she have been able to sniff the deathly scent of the Ublunkyn ice, the issen blauen, and escape it?

"I eventually found my way back. The other bears were astounded when they saw me staggering toward them. They were frightened, of course, when they saw my eyes. But I told them that I might prove useful. At first they didn't believe me. But over the years they have come to trust me. It has worked out well. They hunt for me, and I guard for them during the roarings."

"We're going to the roaring ourselves," Second explained. "We're ready to become hunters!"

Moon Eyes shook his head. "I sense you're hungry, but this is not a place for young cubs. Not during these dark days." The bitterness in his voice reminded First of how disgusted their mother had been by the strange bear who had stolen their seal. "A few seal breathing holes opened up two leagues from here. I can hear their breathing. I can hear the sound of the water welling up in the holes." He lifted one paw and pointed.

"But what about the roaring?" Second asked. She pointed in the opposite direction. "Why can't we hunt with the other bears?"

"Cub!" Moon Eyes said sternly. "What is your name?"

"We haven't been named yet," First said quietly. For the first time, he felt a sense of shame for his nameless condition. If one had a mum, there was really no need for a name. They were Svenna's cubs. That was enough. But now there was no Svenna. No mum. They were nameless and lost. "I'm First, and my sister is Second."

"Ah, of course. I should have known. I shall not ask what happened to your mother, but I assume it was not good. Yes, you need to hunt, but not at the roaring. The bears there won't take kindly to the appearance of two cubs." He paused; then, turning toward the roaring, he sniffed the air. "I sense the issen blauen coming from that direction. There are Roguers out there. Roguers from the Ice Cap."

Then, rising to his full height, he let out a freakish bellowing that seemed to make the moon itself tremble in its transit and shake every star in the sky until the constellations wobbled and the Great Bear appeared to gallop across the night.

CHAPTER 9

Cubs in a Jam

The cubs, heeding Moon Eyes's advice, headed in the opposite direction from the roaring. They did not move fast, however. The mice hadn't done much to diminish their hunger, and they were weak. "Can you even remember the taste of the seals our mum caught?" Second asked her brother as they scrambled over a stretch of spectacularly jumbled ice.

"It was . . . it was . . ." He shook his head. "I can't remember. And I'm too tired to talk."

Then how will we hunt? Second wondered. They didn't only need to eat today. They needed to eat every day, or come spring and summer, when the ice melted and food sources dwindled, during the times of the starving moons, they would die. They had already lost a lot of weight. Neither one of them would have enough fat on them to last through the Dying Ice Moons.

After they'd left Moon Eyes, a smothering fog had rolled in and swallowed the night into an endless sea of gray. It was impossible to find Nevermoves in such conditions. The star was tucked away like a secret in the fleece of the long gray night.

After what felt like hours, they arrived at an expanse of smooth ice that was not buckled up by the mountainous slabs. It would offer a much better view of breathing holes if there were any. "Moon Eyes said there was more than one hole, didn't he, First?"

"Yes," First answered wearily. None was immediately visible. They were so tired, however, that neither cub could take another step. The wind had formed a soft pile of snow that was as inviting to them as their mum's lap — except of course it was not Mum, just snow. They collapsed and fell into a deep sleep. By the time they awakened, the sliver of light that was called day had passed again and the night was new, sparkling with stars. They immediately found Nevermoves. However, the two little stars seemed to have looped back again and were now behind the heel of their mother star, Svenna.

"I think," Second said slowly, "that we have come a fair distance. We are on different ice now." She dug her claws into the ice and brought a clawful of it close to her face, then peered deeply. "I never saw ice like this when we were with Mum. The crystals have a different pattern because we're on a different part of the Frozen Sea. I couldn't build a slide for skeeters here. Too brittle. Too dry. But look over there. That crack!"

"That's a *chukysh*, I think," First said. "Mum told us about them. She said they were narrow trails of open water and there are often lots of fish swimming through them."

"Exactly. There were none where we lived with Mum. But remember she said she'd take us north for them, as there was good fishing and sealing!" Second rose up onto her tiptoes to look at the chukysh. There was a narrow strip of ice-free water. It gleamed like a sparkling ribbon dropped from the night sky, for the water was so black it reflected the stars on its surface.

"But do you think we would really be able to swim it?" First asked nervously. It was tempting, for there was a good chance that it teemed with seals and all sorts of fish. "The currents might be strong, and you know I can't rudder nearly as well as you can, Second."

Something hardened in Second. Why was her brother always so fearful?

"Yes, you can, First! I don't want to hear another word from you about your ruddering. You just have to keep your hind feet flat and focus. Remember, the Great Marven was an ancestor of our father's. And what was he known for?"

"Swimming. He made the fastest passage ever from Point H'Rath in the Northern Kingdoms of Ga'Hoole to Point

Nunqua in the Nunquivik." It sounded like First was speaking more to himself than to Second.

"So no more talk about you ruddering. You just have to concentrate," Second said solemnly.

Their mum often used that word, *concentrate*, and as Second said it aloud, First felt a twinge deep inside him. Like a chunk of jumble ice, it crushed up against his heart. Missing their mum was like a pain that never eased.

First was about to say something when suddenly he caught a familiar whiff. Second caught it too. They both uttered the luscious word. "Seal!"

Quiet as could be, the cubs dropped to their bellies and began to creep forward silently. They were careful not to let their claws click on the ice. They remembered their mum explaining how sounds could be heard much louder under-water. Oh, if only their mum were with them now! But the two cubs knew that this was not the time for mewling.

They were close to the hole now, a shining black disc of water reflecting the stars. They stopped and waited. Second signaled to First, then quietly lifted a paw to cover her nose. Her brother did the same. If a seal came up and saw their glossy black snouts, it would immediately dive into the dark water before bothering to catch a breath.

The hole began to bubble. Something poked up through the froth. At the same time, there was a loud crack and a terrific jolt. The cubs slid across to an edge that hadn't been there before. The ice beneath their paws had broken loose from the vast sheet ice of the Frozen Sea. The swells of the sea rolled under them. Second gripped with her claws. But where was First? She looked over the edge but there was no sign of him. He had simply vanished.

She spotted a dimple in the water nearby that swirled slowly. Had First been sucked down? Where was he? A bear couldn't simply vanish like that. He knew how to swim. But there could be hidden currents. "First! First!" The sky yawned above her. Second had never felt so alone in this vast and empty world.

Then she spied a glittering blade cutting through the water, and her anguish turned to terror.

"Oh no!" Second's throat seemed to close and choke on the word.

Krag shark!

At the same moment, First's head bobbed up in the water.

The krag shark changed its course, heading directly for her brother. The massive sharp teeth gleamed, and a baleful eye looked directly at her brother, as if already savoring the taste of his flesh.

Its eyes are so strange, Second thought. One on each side of its head. *It can't see straight!* With no thought of anything except saving her brother, Second leaped into the water. The shock of the cold momentarily paralyzed her. Her brain locked and her eyeballs seemed to freeze in their sockets and for seconds she could not even breathe.

The shark rolled its head again and changed its direction. How could its prey be in two places at once?

First saw the krag shark turn toward him, lifting its head above the surface. Teeth, that was all he saw. Huge, glistening white teeth. He heard the desperate cry of his sister. But he could not see her. "I'm coming, I'm coming," she called. But what could she do against this monster closing in?

"Dodge, First! Dodge!" Second shouted. Suddenly, First felt a presence stir within him, like a spirit from the Long Ago. *They're stupid beasts, son. Carve the water. You've got the hind paw for it. Feather it. Yes, feather it like a bird on the wing.* And so he feathered his hind paw. The fear began to leak away just a tiny bit. Doing something was better than doing nothing, and it made him bolder. He would outsmart this dumb, savage beast. A mouth without a brain. First had an advantage. *His* eyes faced forward while the shark creature had to keep turning its head to draw First into its sight lines. This was First's advantage, and he was going to play it for all it was worth. He would dart about and confuse the beast. This must be what Second was trying to do as well. Baffle the creature, making it impossible for the shark to focus on either of them.

First saw the confusion in the shark's eye. It was getting tired trying to keep track of both bears, who seemed to be dancing rather than swimming through the Frozen Sea. One would be there, then the other. The shark didn't know which way to turn. It dived deep, then came roaring up, its huge mouth with teeth gleaming fiercely, ready to bite, devour. It rushed forward to where it had last seen a cub. The cubs felt the surge from a great wave of pressure and were actually driven onto the floe. Water washed over them, but they clung with all their might. Their claws dug deep into the ice. They felt the sea bucking beneath the floe and then a stillness.

They turned their heads and looked at each other.

"We're alive!" Second gasped.

"Alive!" First murmured.

"And, First?"

"What?"

"I don't ever want to hear you complain about ruddering again."

"I don't know what happened, Second. It was so mysterious. It was like a spirit filled me . . . like . . . like the Great Marven."

"Not 'like,' First. You *were* the Great Marven."

"He was just a legend, Second."

"Never say 'just' and 'legend' together, brother. Remember what Mum told us once?"

"Yes, I remember now . . . 'Legends' are what you call stories that have died. But if you can bring them back, by telling them over and over again, they become real."

"You brought the legend back, First!"

They clambered across the ice. The sea had calmed now beneath the floe. The breathing hole was still there. But where was the seal?

CHAPTER 10

More Than Prey

They waited patiently on the floe through the rest of the night, wondering if the hole would ever bubble again. They sensed seals all around them. Why would not at least one poke its head up? After several hours, they were almost ready to give up. But they were fearful of getting back into the water, for the floe was no longer connected to the larger ice sheet. It would not be a long swim, but the memory of the krag shark and its nightmarish teeth were still vivid in their minds.

Second felt First give her a sharp nudge. He put his paw to his mouth to signal quiet as something stirred in the water beneath the ice. There was the soft sound of bubbling, and a snout poked up.

"Now!" Second croaked joyfully.

They jammed their paws into the hole at the same time.

Second felt the sea currents sucking on her claws, and yet she was grasping nothing. She tried to reach to the side, but her shoulders were jammed against her brother's. They could hardly wiggle. The ice had a lock on them.

"You're in the way!" Second roared. "Move!"

"*You* move!" he said, trying to wrench away.

Second's frustration turned to panic. "We're stuck, First! I can't get my paw out!"

"Me neither," First gasped. "Pull harder, Second."

"I can't. You have to. Your paw is bigger. I can't pull because yours is in the way."

"Can you wriggle yours?"

"I'll try," Second replied. If she could just angle her paw a bit more . . .

Suddenly, First felt Second's fingers grasping his desperately. "What are you doing?"

"It's back! Except . . . except . . . there's more than one! The krag shark. It's brought its . . . its friends!"

The cubs were transfixed as they gazed at the advancing silvery blades that cut through the water. "Great Ursus!" Second squealed. *We're perfect targets!* she thought, imagining the sharp teeth of the krags slicing off their paws. The closest shark rolled slightly, just as before. A sinister eye appeared again, as if checking its course, then turned white as it slid back into its head.

"Look over there!" Second said in a strangled voice.

"Killer whales," First said weakly. "We're bait. Live bait for every predator in the Nunquivik sea. All because of this cursed hole." He began to shake with fear, but he clasped his sister's paw even tighter. They would die together.

Another voice called out from behind them.

"Do exactly what I say and I might be able to save you. Which is more than you have ever done for my kind."

Whose kind? First wondered. The cubs twisted their heads around to look.

On the edge of the chunk of ice was a seal. He was quite small and had a blue tinge to his pelt.

"How did you get there?" Second asked. They were surrounded by open water, and a herd of very large creatures flashing white bellies were now circling the floe. "Those . . . are . . . are . . ." Second's voice began to quaver.

"Yes, indeed, killer whales," the seal said calmly, almost indifferently. "Orcas, they call themselves." Then, tipping his head, the seal remarked, "And that one, the biggest, is the papa of the pod, I reckon. That's why the krag sharks aren't coming any closer. But if the whales get bored, they might."

The seal yawned. "I'll just clamber up on this floe. I'll be safe. Sorry, can't guarantee what will happen to your paws. They will be a temptation to the krag sharks if the whales get tired and swim away. You know the other name for krag sharks?"

"What?" First asked tremulously.

"The Devil's Blade."

"Oh thank you, thank you for sharing that with us," Second said scathingly. "You're just a bundle of useful information, you little blue creep." She burst into tears, then stopped crying suddenly when, with her paw stuck in the breathing hole, she felt a change in the flow of water. The water was parting for a shark. It was coming closer, his blade cutting through.

A painful realization pushed through the haze of fear. Second was never going to meet her father. *I love you, Da, I love you.* She closed her eyes and tried to imagine him. If she was going to die, she would die thinking of the father she never knew and the mum she loved. First managed to grasp his sister's paw with his own stuck paw. He squeezed it as best he could. Second squeezed back. They would be here with each other until the end.

"I suppose," the seal said in a drawling voice, "you think you're the only victims here. But guess what? I can be eaten by both of you. I'm your favorite food. Remember? I'm sharing an ice floe with my number one predator. You two!"

"What are they doing now?" First yelped as waves began to wash over the ice floe.

"A clever little strategy," the seal replied. "You see, it's a pod — six, maybe seven, killer whales. They start swimming in circles to tip the ice floe. They hope to wash me off, and you as well. What a feast they'll have! Seal with a serving of cubs. The sharks will pick over the leftovers if there are any."

The floe tilted suddenly, and the seal skidded across the ice and slammed into Second. Grasping the cub's tail with his mouth, the seal clamped his flipper onto First's hind paw.

"What can we do?" Second said desperately, her eyes flashing with terror.

"Hard to talk with all this fur in my mouth," the seal mumbled. "I'll try not to bite, but if you'd let me hang on as best I can, I won't slip off. The orcas might get bored and swim away. I think you're safely anchored there with your paws jammed in that hole. Although they might prove too tempting for the krag sharks."

"But if they do swim away, are we stuck here forever?" First asked.

"That depends," the seal answered, though the words were still muffled through the fur. The ice floe was lurching back and forth.

"Depends on what?" Second asked. Her frustration was growing. She and her brother were on the brink of death, and this seal was chatting away almost as if he enjoyed their predicament.

"You be my anchor here. Let me stay on, and if I get you free when these orcas give up and leave, you won't eat me."

"But you're our main supply of food. We need to get fat," First said, shooting a worried glance at Second, who was glaring at the seal.

"Well, I'm also your main supply of brains. So you better let me live. Once these creatures go away, I can guide you to some really fine eating. You'll get fat, I promise."

"What is it?" First said warily. The creature was amazingly strong for a young seal. The pressure of his flipper on First's hind paw was impressive.

"Beluga."

"Oh yeah, right!" Second snorted. "You think my brother and I can take on a *beluga*?"

The water had started to calm. One of the pod had become bored, just as the seal had predicted.

"You don't have to 'take on' the beluga," the seal replied. "It's already dead. Got caught high on dry land between tides. The carcass is up there at the very end of the channel, or what we call a tickle in these parts. She died just last night. I know about her, but so far no bears know. I could lead you there." He paused and looked out beyond the floe they were on toward the ice-free water. "Look, the last orca just left. I told you they were easily bored. And the krag sharks seem to be following. But if I lead you to the beluga, there's one condition."

"We agree not to eat you," First said.

"I know it sounds hard. But I think you will learn to like me. I have character."

"What does that mean?" Second asked, narrowing her eyes.

"It means I am not simply blubber. I have an honest nature.

I can be more than prey for you, and I recognize that you are more than simply killers."

"We prefer 'predators,'" First explained.

"Call it what you will. The outcome is the same. I die a violent death and your hunger is satisfied."

"You seem to be forgetting one tiny little thing," Second said. "Our paws are stuck in this hole."

"I can dive into the water and cause a commotion under my breathing hole. It will loosen your paws." The seal paused. "Or I could just swim off. There will be no wind tonight to stir things up. Who knows; by tomorrow, new ice might form. Then you'd really be frozen in. Or perhaps a shark might come back and snap off your paws. Or a toothwalker. The choice is yours. Beluga in the tickle, or ice locked here?"

CHAPTER 11

Up the Tickle

The commotion worked. The cubs' paws slid easily from the ice hole. First stuck his paw in his mouth and began sucking on it, then removed it and stared as if it was a miracle that the paw was still attached.

"Thank you," Second murmured. She looked up at the seal, who'd climbed back onto the floe. He was prey and she had been predator, but everything had changed. She tried not to wonder whether his blubber would be tasty.

"You saved us!" First said. "I can't tell you how grateful we are. What can we do for you? Whatever you ask."

Second gave her brother a sharp look, as though to say, *Have some pride. Someday we'll be the largest predators on earth, and we've already promised not to eat the seal.*

But First was still yammering away. "Without our paws we are nothing."

"Well, not exactly *nothing*, First," his sister interjected before turning to the seal. "We don't even know your name. What is it?"

The seal looked at them for several seconds. This was a problem. Seal names were long, complex strings of sounds that were nearly inaudible under the ice to other creatures. According to tradition, real names were never spoken above ice, though some seals did have an "above-ice name." But this was the first time this seal had ever been asked. He paused to think before a word finally popped into his head. It was the name of a sunken ship, a ship from the time of the Others, that rested on a rock ledge in the bay near a river mouth.

"S. S. Jameson," he barked proudly. "I mean, Jameson. And what's yours?"

"Oh, we don't have names yet," First replied.

Jameson slapped his flipper onto the ice flow. It rocked slightly. "I forgot. I find that habit despicable. You should have names. Every creature on earth deserves a name. No matter how big or small."

"But we have no one to name us," First said.

"Are you orphans?" Jameson asked.

"No!" Second stamped her paw. "Our father has gone to

the far north country to hunt with the male bears. And we are going to join him."

"You want to hunt with the male bears?" The seal looked at Second doubtfully.

"Of course," Second said, tossing her head.

"Our mum had to leave to go on a noble mission," First said proudly. "But she'll come back. She loves us. She just had to go."

Jameson cocked his head. "What kind of a mission? I mean, other than noble?"

First took a deep breath. "She's been called to the Den of Forever Frost. It's the most important place in the history of bears."

Jameson looked blankly at them. He seemed as ignorant of the den as Lago had been.

"It's real!" Second said, stamping her paw again.

"I never said it wasn't," Jameson responded amiably. "Nevertheless, you still need names. Think about it while we swim up the tickle."

The cubs exchanged a glance. First saw the doubt in his sister's eyes. Did she have the same question he had? Why was it that the two times they had mentioned their mum going to the Den of Forever Frost, both creatures had seemed doubtful? But why else would their mum leave them? Despite his anxiety, First kept his fears to himself. It was too frightening to think that their mum had left them for no reason at all.

"You mean we should name ourselves?" First asked.

"Who else is going to do it?" Jameson swiveled his head around. "Come this way. It's not that far from here to the tickle."

They plunged into the water and swam after Jameson, nervously glancing behind them for any of the glittering blades of the krag sharks.

Deep layers of pale purple left from dusk washed the sky. At this time of year, the day clung to its colors at both dawn and dusk. It was as if the sun that had slid away to another world still wanted to leave some of its cloth of light behind. The haunting blues and the bruised lavenders remained. The stars appeared brighter against this cloth as the cubs swam behind the seal. The bear constellation was beginning to climb high into the night.

"Look!" Second said, stroking the water gently as she swam, then rolling onto her back for a better view of the sky. "There's Jytte and Stellan."

"Oh! They're skipping ahead now," First said. He too had turned on his back and begun to float.

"How come some stars become unstuck?" Second asked.

"It's a mystery," Jameson replied quietly. He was upright and bobbing in the water as he tipped his head back to watch the stars.

"That's what Mum said about Jytte and Stellan," First explained. "A mystery."

Jameson turned his head and whispered, "Do you feel it?"

"Feel what?" Second asked.

"The halibut."

"Halibut!" The cubs gasped and their stomachs rumbled in anticipation of the delicious fish.

"Calm down. Don't scare it off," Jameson warned.

"So you're going to catch him?" First asked.

"He's too big for me." Jameson turned and swam toward them. "But just the right size for you. I'll give you a tip. Halibut are slow swimmers, bottom swimmers. It's not all that deep here. No time like the present to try. Now down you go; I'll coach you. Just remember, you're hunters."

The seal is right, Second thought. *We are hunters. But Mum taught us about hunting on ice, not diving beneath it.*

First felt panic swell within him as he thought about the dive. He would have to angle his hind paws just right. That was his weak point, angling his paws in the water. Second was so much better.

Second recalled what Mum said about breathing underwater, not to inhale but to blow bubbles out, or their lungs would fill up with water and they would drown. *Not happening*, Second thought. *We are not going to drown!*

First seemed to read her mind about drowning. He looked at her nervously. "I don't mean to sound dismal, sister, but . . ."

"But you already do!" Second said. "And there's no reason for it. Just remember, you have to stop blowing bubbles when you close in on prey, or the bubbles will give you away. Now stop worrying. You're always thinking of reasons why things won't work. We can do this!" Second was growing tired of her brother's worries. "You can't let your worries eat you. You must eat the worries and be done with them." She paused as a thought came to her. "Remember how Mum told us the story about the Great Marven."

"Oh, the legendary Great Marven," Jameson broke in. "Greatest swimming bear ever during the time of the Great Melting. Killed more dragon walruses than any other Nunquivik bear. More seals too."

"You know about Marven?" First asked. He was surprised that such stories could come down through the ages, and that another creature of a very different kind could know about them.

"I do," Jameson replied. "We grew up with such stories. Though no one talks about them much anymore." A light sparkled in Jameson's eyes. "I can smell him. We're closing in on that halibut."

The shadow of the fish loomed ahead. As they drew closer, they were relieved to see that the halibut, although a husky fellow, was not nearly as big as the orcas. Jameson began making strange whistles that they didn't understand, pointing this way and that with his flippers and head. The cubs dived and closed their mouths. No bubbles! The halibut moved very slowly and seemed confused by the two cubs and the seal. As First approached the halibut from the side, he realized what Jameson had been trying to signal to them. *Get the fish to roll.*

Second swam up close and made a swiping movement that stirred the water, but she did not touch the fish. The halibut started to roll slightly. Instinctually, First went in for the fish's belly while Second whacked the fish's back with her paw, breaking its spine. Jameson let out a shrill squeal and clapped his flippers as the cubs dragged the halibut to the surface.

"Oh Great Ursus!" First exclaimed. "I can't believe it! We did it. We did it! My hind paws worked, worked again, just like Great Marven."

"See!" Second said, glad to see her brother pleased with himself.

"Quick now," Jameson coached them. "Get him out before others come and take a chunk out of him. What a fatty this fellow is!"

"Where can we put him?" Second asked.

"On the edge of the tickle. There's enough room for all of us."

The cubs clambered onto the rim of the tickle, dragging their catch. The redolent smell of the fish seemed to make the air quiver. It'd been so long since they'd eaten properly.

Second was just about to tear off a chunk of the tender flesh, but managed to stop herself. "No, you first — not you, First. I mean Jameson."

"Of course," First said. *This is exactly why we need names! Too confusing.*

After Jameson had his first bite, the cubs began feasting on the tender, flaky flesh. They ate and ate until only the bones of the fish were left. Their bellies were filled at last, and for the first time in days they felt satisfied.

Sprawled on the ice rim of the tickle, his paws clasped over his belly, First looked up at the sky. The big bear constellation was just clambering over the horizon. First waited patiently for the hind legs to appear and then began to search for his mum's star in the heel, and then his father's star in the knee. The sky seemed to arc so low over them that First felt if he stood tall enough he might reach out and pluck these stars from the night. They were so close, he could almost hear the stars whispering to him.

"Second," he said quietly, "I have an idea. I think we should name ourselves."

Second blinked at her brother. Could they really do that? What would they name themselves?

They each wondered silently for just a second or two; then they rolled up onto their knees, tipped their heads to the sky, and spied those two wandering stars. They knew in a twinkle what their names should be.

"I'm Jytte and no longer Second."

"And I'm Stellan and no longer First."

"It seems right, doesn't it?" said Second, who was now Jytte.

"It seems very right to me!" Jameson chimed in, clapping his flippers in delight.

"Yes, it does sound right, but I'm not quite sure why," Stellan said.

"I'll tell you why, Stellan."

"Why, Jytte?" They loved saying their brand-new names.

"It's because those two stars are following our da, and we can too!" She said this firmly as her eyes looked at the star called Svern, their father's star. "Remember what Mum said? His name is Svern, and that's the star in the hind knee . . ."

Stellan broke in, " 'The same leg as my heel star,' Mum said. 'You see, we walk together across the sky. Heel follows knee.' "

And so they were named.

Suddenly, the sky seemed to flinch, and then the dome of the night began to dance with color. Stellan tipped his head to the undulating hues. It was almost as if each color was raining down upon his pelt. His guard hairs were tipped in violets and starlit greens and rose. Was it possible to feel color? He looked at his sister. Her guard hairs shimmered as well, like she was part of a rainbow. Magic was happening.

"Jytte, is this magic, or —"

"It's the *ahalikki!*" Jytte shouted in delight. Jameson looked up too. The white fur of the cubs' pelts glowed with color, while his own sleek black coat seemed only to soak up the light. But still he felt it and basked in this night as the cubs began to rise to their feet.

The cubs had seen these lights once before with their mum. The luminous ribbons of color unfurled across the darkness silently. Then the ribbons began to pulse, and soon waves of crimson and orange flowed through the night. All perfectly silent. And yet the lights appeared to dance to a music of their own, a hidden music that belonged to eternity. The cubs basked in this palette of the sky. Sometimes their white fur was tinged with lavender or blue or the softest pink. The cubs felt driven to rise on their hind legs and join the dance to this elusive music of the sky. Jameson watched, wishing, so wishing, that he had feet.

The ahalikki seemed like a blessing of sorts from the sky in celebration of their new names. Was it possible, Jameson thought, that he and these cubs could become friends even though they were such different kinds?

CHAPTER 12

The Ice Clock

The ice chimes were ringing the hour. Svenna had been here for a week, and in that time, the ache in her heart for her cubs had not diminished one bit.

This place, called the Ice Cap, was the strangest place she had ever been. Svenna gazed out the ice hole in the ceiling of her den. In the frosty air the big clock glowered. It was immense, standing taller than the biggest fir trees back in the Northern Kingdoms of Ga'Hoole. But unlike a real tree, it bristled with rods, strange spirals, and queer little springs and screws. Sheathed in clear ice, the metal parts gleamed night and day.

The shining crystal orb of issen blauen covered a "face," a white disc on which numerals had been inscribed. There were long, pointy gold sticks, thin as whiskers but called hands, that moved around the disc.

A new bell began to chime. It was the Summoning Chime calling the bears to the Formularium, where they gathered once a day to chant before the clock. Svenna got up and walked from her den to join the other bears, who were streaming from the various ice corridors into the Formularium.

The ceremony was presided over by the Mystress of the Hands, a rather corpulent, squat bear whose paws were adorned with golden sticks, like those of the clock.

There were perhaps fifty bears in the Formularium, and as they entered, they all kneeled and began to sway in time with the swing of the pendulum.

"Repeat after me!" the Mystress of the Hands called out as she swung the golden sticks on her paws.

There were dire consequences for those who did not chant properly. Special bears, monitors with extremely big ears and acute hearing, threaded through the congregation. At least once during every service, Svenna saw one of these bears yank a lower-ranking bear from its knees, presumably for making a mistake while chanting.

Svenna never saw those bears again.

The Mystress of the Hands's melodious voice filled the vast Formularium.

"Almighty Clock, protect us always from the demon melting waters

May your gears and paddles turning
Save us from perdition
Let the faithful be rewarded
When the last chime tolls
Repent, repent, those who stray
And take our humble Tick Tock offering
And spare us from the last most dreadful day
We asked this in the name of the Highest Authority
The Grand Patek."

Although Svenna had heard this chant countless times since her arrival, the words never ceased to make her shiver. This was not how bears were supposed to act. These strange rituals were not like the hunting laws intended to prevent prey from suffering unnecessarily. Nor were they the sort of laws that banned hunting char during the moon of the halibut, for that was when the char could cause sickness. These rituals were meant to prevent another Great Melting, but how was that possible? What could a *clock* do to keep the waters at bay?

As always, while the Mystress of the Hands spoke the last words, the Grand Patek entered, accompanied by his guard to recite the Creed of the Ice Clock.

Despite his lavish adornments, which included a shimmering ice crown and a shield studded with luminous rocks as bright as the lights of the ahalikki, nothing could disguise his battle scars. His body was striped with black from where the fur had been ripped away in a lifetime of ferocious battles. One ear had been torn off, and the crown sat at an odd angle on his head.

"The nonbelievers shall be ferreted out. Every second that ticks away, every tock of our clock will bring us closer to the truth. The blood has been sacrificed, and the clock, all-knowing, drinks that blood and makes all that was torn apart whole again. So it is that one cub is taken, and one is left behind to perish. The serpent of evil shall drown. The angels of the Ice Clock shall rise."

Svenna felt a stitch in her heart every time she heard those words: "One cub is taken, and one is left behind to perish." She still didn't know why the Roguers stole cubs and brought them here. But there were dark rumors about how the cubs, known as the Tick Tocks, were used in the great Ice Clock.

The next portion of the ritual was the changing of the cubs. The guards removed two cubs from the wide pans that were part of a balance mechanism in the clock, attached to an unseen mechanism known as the wheel.

As always, they were thin and scarred. Was this what her own cubs, First and Second, would have been doing if she had not offered to serve in their place?

Svenna's stomach churned as she watched the guards take the cubs away. This was not how bears were supposed to live — cooped up all together. Chanting instead of hunting. Stealing innocent cubs from their mums. She knew she wouldn't last long in this terrible place. She had to find a way out before then. She had to make it back to her cubs, by any means necessary.

CHAPTER 13

The Toothwalker

"Well, cubs, I fear that it is time for me to leave," Jameson said. He'd given the cubs directions to the beluga as promised, though now that the cubs were full of halibut, it felt less urgent.

"You have to leave now?" Jytte asked. "Please stay a bit longer."

"I can't. The tide's running out and the water in the tickle is becoming too low for legless creatures like myself."

"But, Jameson" — Stellan looked into the shining dark eyes of the seal — "how can we ever thank you? You saved our lives."

"I know. Strange, isn't it? Prey saving a predator's life."

"We'll never eat you!" Jytte blurted out.

"Never ever," Stellan said.

"I know that," Jameson said softly. "We're friends now. True friends."

Friends. The word had a wondrous sound, Stellan thought.

"And so, my friends, good-bye." Jameson reached out with his flippers and patted each of the cubs, then slipped into the water.

He began swimming away but kept turning his head back, making tremulous whistling sounds that the cubs supposed meant good-bye. They kept waving until the seal was out of sight. Jytte turned to Stellan. "It always seems we're waving good-bye to someone — first it was Mum and then it was Lago, and now Jameson."

And now to ourselves, Stellan thought. As they stood on their hind legs in knee-deep water with their new names, Stellan experienced the peculiar sensation that they were also waving farewell to First and Second, the cubs they had once been. It was as if those cubs were fading into the gloaming of the endless night of the Nunquivik.

"Jytte, we can't think about good-bye now. We're going to find Da. We need to keep heading north, to those hunting grounds. We'll watch for those Roguers. We'll be careful."

They swam on, often tipping their heads up to see the star that never moved, and the two smaller stars that once again had skipped ahead. Could these three stars guide them and protect them? They were approaching land, they could tell. In the night they spied a fringe of small trees like pale shadows. They were called white barks, and they grew in scattered patches, often at the edge of the Frozen Sea, where slender limbs swayed in the slightest breeze and their leaves in summer often made a soft, whispering music. Now, as the moon began to set low in the sky, the trees turned silvery. The water in the tickle was perfectly calm and the reflection from the ahalikki cast pools of color. It was like swimming though a liquid rainbow.

As they approached the end of the tickle, they could see the carcass of the beluga shimmering like a great white stone on the beach. The water was at half tide now and rising, but alas, too late for the whale.

Suddenly, they heard a sound skidding toward them from a ridge of jumble ice that rimmed the tickle. A huge and hideous face hung down from the ridge. It must have climbed out farther down where the water was still deep, as this end of the tickle was almost completely dry. The face had two long, glaring tusks and a nose encrusted with prickly hairs.

"No passing! The whale is for me," it roared.

It was a beast so huge that he blotted out the sky. Stellan felt a coldness creep over him. It was different from any kind of cold he had ever felt. It was paralyzing. There was something terrible and freakish about the beast's eyes. They were not forward facing, but appeared to have slid off to each side of its head, and they were a dark red, like old blood. The bristly hairs on its face twitched with a life of their own.

The cubs were so frightened they couldn't think. They couldn't move. It felt as if their very guts were climbing up into their throats as they watched the drool drip from the creature's mouth. *We're about to be devoured*, Stellan thought. Their mum had told them how dangerous and vicious these monsters were.

"Toothwalkers," their mum had said, "prefer cub flesh to any other. As hunters, their habits are horrible. All of their prey suffer and die slowly, for they like to watch the fear in their eyes."

Stellan felt his fear radiating from him, arousing the toothwalker's hunger. Long ropes of saliva were dripping from its mouth.

"I smell halibut!" the creature said. A disgusting, mottled tongue slipped from its mouth. "Halibut, freshly digested. And if I eat you, I get the halibut as well! But I shall eat you slowly. I shall rip open your stomach and take the halibut and then eat your heart. A heart eaten while still beating is juicy."

Heart grit! thought Stellan. *I've dodged a shark, jumped on the back of a skunk bear. We can do this. We can do this.* The words unleashed a surge of strength, propelling Stellan as he leaped up and bit the mottled tongue of the toothwalker. The creature yowled. Blood sprayed into the night as the beast rolled onto its back, flailing helplessly with its flippers at the sky.

"Run!" Stellan yelled to Jytte. "Run toward the whale before the tide comes in." They had to. They could outrun a toothwalker, but not outswim one. The water they were standing in was shallow, but quickly becoming deeper. With each second they were losing their advantage over the toothwalker, who was now howling in anger more than pain. The cubs pushed mightily on the gritty bottom of the tickle and sprang forward, sailing through the air toward the beach where the beluga carcass lay. But just then, the toothwalker swung its head wildly, trying to right himself onto its belly. The long tusks flashed through the air, and Stellan felt something strike his haunch. He kept running for a few seconds, but then he couldn't. A sharp pain coursed through him. His sister screamed.

"You're bleeding, Stellan!" Jytte had seen the tusk slice into her brother. His blood splattered her face. A hot fury flashed through her, unleashing a surge of power. She thought of nothing, not fear, not danger, not blood. She would die, but she would die killing if she had to. She wheeled around and, grabbing her brother, dragged him by his front paw out of the range of the toothwalker's long tusks. She was startled by her own strength. She wondered if suddenly the power of her father, Svern, had swept through her, overtaken her, if only for that single moment.

"You're all right. You're all right, Stellan. Look, there's not much blood. It was just the shock of it all that was probably the worst."

Stellan blinked at his sister, looking at her in wonder. "Jytte, do you realize what you just did? You're smaller than me and you dragged me all this way. The toothwalker can't reach us. Look at it over there. It's still on the ice, on its back."

Jytte's eyes opened wide. "I guess I did, but . . . but it didn't feel like me."

"It *was* you, Jytte. You saved my life."

The toothwalker was now bellowing, a raw, searing sound of pure rage. It tried to clamber across the ice, but its flippers were useless. "Mine, mine!" it kept railing into the night as the moon dragged in the tide.

The beluga was just where Jameson had promised. The meat was not as tender as the halibut. They had to work hard to get it, tearing through the thick skin, but it was worth it. Stellan kept glancing at the moon, which was rising.

"We need to eat fast," he said. "If the water reaches the beluga, the toothwalker will come with it."

"Is the water coming closer?" Jytte dared not look around but kept eating the whale flesh.

"No, it can't. We're safe until the tickle fills in. The tooth-walker can't make it to us across this ice. We're far enough."

Jytte stopped gorging and lifted her muzzle toward the sky. Her mother's voice echoed in her mind: *A young moon is a strong moon, a tide dragger.* A sliver of a new moon scraped the dark, and the lap of the water on the incoming tide could be heard.

"Eat faster!" Jytte said.

CHAPTER 14

The Numera

When the Mystress of the Hands learned that Svenna could read and write, she'd assigned Svenna to the Numera. That first day, Svenna had been led to a large room where she'd seen row upon row of bears hunched over ice-slab desks, scribbling on ice tablets. Vryk, a bear known as a preceptor, a kind of teacher, had greeted her in a clipped, expressionless tone.

"This is the Numera. We calculate here."

"Calculate what?" Svenna had asked.

Vryk had looked at her blankly. "Information from the clock can help prepare us for the next Great Melting." Svenna felt a shiver course through her. *How could that be possible?*

The Great Melting had been the most cataclysmic event in the history of bears. Not only had thousands of bears perished in the floods, but it had unleashed the monstrous dragons that swam in the depths of the sea.

"How can mere calculations prepare us for the next Great Melting?"

Vryk appeared stunned by the question. "Keep your musings to yourself!" he said sharply.

"It was a question, not a musing."

"Questions are not welcome here. Doubt is not welcome here. Doubt is punishable. Severely punishable."

Svenna's only real question was how long would she have to be here until she could return to her cubs. She asked herself this question a hundred times a day. Her purpose on earth was to raise those dear cubs. To teach them how to hunt, how to swim, how to be honorable bears who knew their own history, and not to sit in front of this abacus recalculating endless columns of figures.

Soon a gong sounded, and then the first of the quarter chimes. This was the signal for the evening meal.

"Time for lineup," her denmate Hanne said cheerfully. She was a female about Svenna's age, perhaps a bit older.

Like everything at the Ice Cap, meals in the ice dining hall, a vast space with many tunnels leading off it, were carefully choreographed. Bears entered the hall from a designated tunnel according to their service, and always in a prescribed order. From one of the ice balconies a young bear took her place at the ice harp. The frame of the harp was made from the special-quality ice known as *frysenglass*. The strings were made from the hollow guard hairs shed from bears, which gave a haunting resonance when they were plucked. The first chords signaled the entrance of the bears in the highest echelons of the High Council of the Timekeepers.

Next came the High Chamber of the Prefects, followed by the Low Chamber of the Prefects. Svenna took her place now in the O'Clock Tunnel, as it was called, where the numerators lined up. A new sequence of chimes had begun sounding the hour, and on the second stroke of the chimes, her line began to move into the dining hall. At the same time from the Works Tunnel came the guards, the Roguers, the hunters, and the greasers, who, with whale oil, would lubricate the various moving parts of the clock. Svenna noticed that in contrast to the hunters and the Roguers, the greasers were quite thin and generally smaller than full-grown bears. Also from the Works Tunnel came dozens of very small seals with a bluish cast.

Lastly came the Order of Tick Tocks. They were all cubs, and they entered from behind a swaying curtain of icicles at the back of the hall at the very lowest tables.

"What do they use those cubs for?" Svenna asked Hanne.

"They have devoted their lives to the clock. It is a great honor."

Svenna stared at the small, trembling creatures. "But did they make that choice themselves?"

Hanne gave her a puzzled look. "What does it matter?"

What does it matter? Svenna thought, horrified. If these cubs had indeed been taken against their will, then nothing could matter more. They were supposed to be with their mums, learning to swim, to hunt. Not stuck here, being paraded about as part of some ridiculous charade. Part of her wanted to run to them, grab as many as she could, and flee this strange, terrible place. But the guards would surely kill her, and then there would be no one to care for her own cubs.

With a sigh, Svenna tried to turn her attention to her dinner. She found the food at the Ice Cap odd. She had never heard of food being "prepared." What preparation was needed beyond hunting? Once you found your prey, you killed it, tore off chunks of succulent meat, and ate it. Here, however, instead of hunting, food was "prepared" some distance away at the twin volcanoes Pupya and Prya. So everything they ate had the peculiar odor.

At the high tables, the elite bears known as the Authority were seated. They were given a choice for their meat of *smutz y bludder* — smoked or bloody. At the lowest table it was all bludder.

Hanne was craning her neck for a glimpse of the Mystress of the Chimes. "They are taking their places now. You have a much better view since you've been promoted and get to sit with me at this table."

"I see the Master of the Complications," said Svenna. He was a very large bear with a slight limp.

"Yes, and above him is the Chronos," Hanne said.

Finally, as the music of the ice harp reached a crescendo, the Grand Patek entered. He was carried on the Frost Throne by the four largest bears of the Timekeepers' high guard, the Issengard. These bears' massive chests were always emblazoned with the fresh blood of a beluga whale whose blubber would be smoked for the next meal. The blood itself streaked down their chests on a diagonal like a banner. It was similar to the bloody badges of the Roguers who had come for Svenna, but more ostentatious. These were proud, arrogant bears.

All the highest-ranking bears were festooned with the jewelry of timepieces. Some, like the Mystress of the Chimes, wore tiny springs hanging from their ears. Others jingled with all manner of dials and wheels.

"Can you see the Mystress of the Chimes? Do you see the jewelry she's wearing tonight?" someone whispered.

"Look, see around her neck those blazing stones. The blue ones are sapphires, and then there are the red rubies."

"What do they have to do with clocks?" Svenna asked.

"Not sure, really, but they're very important. They put them in the jewel holes of the clock," Hanne explained.

Another bear, Ragvar, a preceptor in the Numera, leaned toward Svenna. "Bearings," he said. "They bear the friction and make the gear trains run smoothly. The ones the Mystress wears are just the leftovers from which the clock jewels were cut."

Svenna was left dizzy by what she was seeing and hearing. This was a world she never could have dreamed of. A hideous world where mechanical things were worshipped. Where bloody badges and black scars had become adornments along with jewels, while young cubs were enslaved and abused. Nothing she saw had anything to do with the noble traditions of the bears, traditions that had been passed from generation to generation from the days of the first bear council in the Den of Forever Frost. *These creatures don't have the right to call themselves bears*, she thought, looking around in disgust. She was trapped in a living nightmare.

CHAPTER 15

Ghost Town

No sooner had Stellan and Jytte stepped onto land near the fringe of silvery trees than a thick fog began to roll in. It grew thicker and thicker.

"I've never seen anything like this," Jytte said as they started walking. Were they getting closer to the hunting grounds? She sensed they were getting farther from the sea. It was a dry fog and did not have the sting of salt. But it grew steadily thicker. And when did night end and morning begin? In the dense murk of the void between sky and earth, it seemed to be truly no place. Without the stars, they felt adrift. It was almost dizzying, and even with their four paws on the ground, it was hard to tell up from down, as sky and land seemed to merge. They trudged on through the frightening infinity of the void.

At last they were so tired they curled up and fell fast asleep. The fog was still thick when Stellan woke. Starting to rise up, he struck his head something on hard.

"Ouch!" he cried.

Jytte was instantly awake. "What in the world . . . ?" Stellan was muttering and squinting at something. Jytte blinked. "What are you looking for? You can't see a thing. This fog is thicker than Mum's belly fur."

"I'm just trying to see what's in front of my face right here."

"What is it?"

"It's . . . letters! Letter on a piece of wood." He yanked the wood up from the deep snow.

"Letters!" Jytte echoed. "Remember Mum was teaching us letters. She said many of the stories from the Long Ago had been written down in the Den of Forever Frost. Let's try and sound it out."

"W-I-N-S-T-O-N." Stellan spelled out the first word. Then the second: "S-N-O-W-T-E-L."

"Win . . . ston Snow-tel? Is that a name? A place?"

"I don't know. But let's keep moving," Stellan said, glancing over his shoulder.

"But what direction?" Jytte swiveled her head. "I can't see anything. I can't even see where we came from. We're supposed to be going north by following the star Nevermoves. But we move all the time, and unless we can see that star we don't really know what direction we're moving in, do we, Stellan?"

"We just have to put one paw in front of the other and go."

So they went. There passed more pieces of wood with letters. WINSTON GAS ALL NIGHT, WINSTON 5&10, and CALL 675-2327 (BEAR).

"Hey," Stellan said. "That word is bear!"

"That's nice. It's like we're being welcomed."

"Welcomed to what? Where are we?" He felt a prick of suspicion. Other creatures did not put up signs to welcome bears.

The fog had not let up. As they headed in what they hoped was a northerly direction, the cubs passed several strange dens. They were all aboveground and made from wood. "How does a bear live here?" Stellan asked, looking about. "Most of these dens don't have roofs. And they have holes, but they aren't round."

The cubs came to call the holes "not rounds" and couldn't figure out why they were in the middle of the wall of a den. But the dens made good shelters, especially as a blizzard had begun to blow in.

"These not rounds, maybe they're here in case the bears want to look out at something," Stellan said.

Jytte was quiet for several moments, then turned to her brother. "You know what, Stellan? I don't think bears really lived here."

"You don't?" A shiver coursed through him, a shiver not of cold but of fear. He didn't want to encounter any more strange creatures — skunk bears, toothwalkers, krag sharks. He'd had enough. "Jytte, if bears didn't live here, who did?"

"It could be the Others."

"Others?" Stellan's voice quaked.

"Maybe. Let's go see," Jytte replied, and walked into the den. She looked around a bit and then tried sitting near a not round.

"These aren't as cozy as a real den," she pronounced. She got up and settled into a corner. "Not cozy at all." She sighed as she looked up into the roofless den, which was now hung with the impenetrable fog. "I want the stars."

I want Mum, Stellan thought, but said nothing.

Jytte looked in vain for the Svern star. Her mum's words flowed through her: *That's the star in the hind knee of the same leg as my heel star. You see, we walk together across the sky. Heel follows knee.* Jytte wondered if perhaps they might be so lucky as to find their father and mother together someday, somewhere.

Later they roused themselves and started out again. And again they walked through the thick pelt of fog and blizzard, heading in the direction they believed was north. They felt their energy dwindling. The cold seemed to pierce right through their fur. Jytte was thinner than Stellan was, and he thought he heard her teeth chattering. A terrible, sad little sound.

"Oh no!" Stellan gasped. "The letters again. The same ones, WINSTON SNOWTEL. We're going in circles!"

"We can't be!" Jytte said. Fury rose within her. It was as if the whole universe was playing a nasty trick on them. She scooped up a pawful of snow. Dry snow. Not good for skeeter slides. They must be a fair distance from the sea and the northern hunting grounds. Bears did not hunt on land in this season. She crinkled her brow and began to think. It was maddening that without the stars they had become lost and merely gone in circles. Her mum had said she was an ice gazer. She had to use what their mum had called her *gift* to find their way again and not go in circles.

"We're going to get out of here," Jytte said firmly.

"How? Where are we going?"

"Not in circles, that's for sure." Stellan felt he could almost see her brain working. "The crystals should change as we get closer to the sea, closer to the tickle."

"Are there crystals that point north to the hunting grounds?"

"Maybe. I'll learn the difference." She'd always used her gift to look for the good snow or ice for slides, or packing snowballs to hurl at her brother, or fragments from a jumble to build a lookout tower. But now she would use this gift to go north to the hunting grounds. North to Da!

And so they continued, very slowly. As they trudged across the snow, Stellan began to sense something shadowing them. He could not pick up a scent, but there was something out there. Was it an Other?

"Jytte, I think something is following us. Maybe an Other."

"Don't be ridiculous. The Others are gone. They died. Died even before the Great Melting."

"*Something* is following us."

"Well, it's not an Other, Stellan."

"Maybe not. But still, something is tracking us. I feel it."

"Feel it?" Jytte turned to look at her brother. "Where do you feel it?"

"In my head. It's . . . it's . . . picking at my brain."

Jytte shivered. She didn't like it when something picked at her brother's brain. It was often something sad, and never good.

CHAPTER 16

"Trust me . . ."

Uluk Uluk chuckled to himself. *They think I'm an Other. My my! But who are these cubs? Uncommonly bright, that's for sure!* The old bear guessed that the she-cub was an ice gazer, for the endless fogs of Winston were normally unnavigable, and she somehow knew that studying the ice and snow crystals would yield more information than peering into the nothingness of the fog. And the other cub, the brother called Stellan, had sensed Uluk Uluk's presence. That cub was a riddler! He could riddle the mind and pick out a creature's thoughts. A stunning pair they made. Could Uluk Uluk bend them to his task? A task that he'd had in mind ever since he had fled the Ice Cap?

He had to hurry back. He would be there to welcome them!

These two young cubs might be the ones he'd been looking for all these long years

The old bear Uluk Uluk had lived in this forsaken place for years. He had fled the Ublunkyn and the Ice Cap at its very top because he saw the clock's noble purpose being perverted. Svree and the owls had built the clock to help *predict* the next Great Melting. The clock was meant to be a tool, and nothing more. But the Grand Patek had encouraged the bears to do more than study the clock; he'd taught them to *worship* it. The Timekeepers had been turned into idolaters, worshipping a mechanical creation — a wondrous one indeed, but not a living one. And what was happening in the name of this false god was horrifying. When he saw the blood on the wheel, the blood of young cubs, he left. His journey had been long and arduous. For some years he went from place to place, settling for only a few moons so the Roguers couldn't find him.

Most creatures avoided these old settlements from the time of the Others, for they were thought to be cursed. But as soon as he stumbled into Winston, he felt safe and knew he would never be found here. He could pursue his dream of destroying the clock. He now circled back the way he had come. He did not want the cubs to be too nervous and would be sure to put out something to lure them. He still had a haunch of caribou left. With the wind blowing from the east, the scent would carry directly to them.

"Jytte!" Stellan blurted suddenly. "Jytte, get your snout out of the snow."

She lifted her head, then gave a small, gleeful bark. "Boo boo meat!"

"Yes, caribou. You smell it too?"

With the east wind, the fog began to rapidly dissolve, revealing a black night spiked with stars. And there was Nevermoves. Uncountable gifts had suddenly rained down upon the cubs all at the same time. Stars, caribou, even a trace of cod. And just ahead was another den. And another sign. BEAR Containment Facility.

The cubs were curious and began to trot toward the den. There were openings, as there had been in the others, but these had sticks with spaces in between.

"What are those?" Jytte exclaimed.

"Bear paws," whispered Stellan, skidding to a stop. "There's a bear behind those bars!"

Two enormous paws were gripping the sticks in one of the openings.

A voice rang out. The whole den seemed to tremble.

"Welcome to jail!"

The cubs froze in their footprints, then clung to each other and rolled into a ball. *Maybe*, thought Stellan, *we'll look like a large lump of snow.*

"It's not a toothwalker," Jytte whispered.

"But what is it?"

"Don't know." Jytte's voice was still trembling, and she clutched her brother even harder.

"Be my guest," the voice called out. "We have a vacancy in cell block number four. Please read the rules before entering the confinement area." The voice paused. They still could not see the entire bear, just his paws on the sticks. His paws were huge, but the claws appeared rather small, as if they had been filed down to splinters.

A sliver of a claw was now pointing. "Can't read them? I'll help you out.

"*DO NOT ENTER.*

DO NOT COME NEAR THE BEARS.

DO NOT TEASE THE BEARS EVEN FROM A DISTANCE.

VIOLATORS OF THE ABOVE RULES WILL BE PROSECUTED TO THE FULL EXTENT OF THE LAW, WITH FINES UP TO FIVE THOUSAND DOLLARS.

"In short" —- the bear shook a claw at them — "scram! But that doesn't apply to you cubs. It was meant for the Others. They're long gone, of course."

Stellan pressed his muzzle to his sister's ear. "Jytte, he could be one of those . . . those Roguer bears."

The bear now revealed himself as he lowered to all fours and ambled through a large opening where part of the wall had collapsed.

Jytte and Stellan were stunned. Never in their short lives had they seen a more raggedy bear. He was tall but painfully thin, so thin that his pelt puddled around his feet like white, curling waves breaking on a beach. He seemed very frail and walked with a decided limp. But the oddest thing of all was that over one eye there was a circular piece of issen blauen, the kind that had been packed into Moon Eyes's sockets. But this piece was attached to a delicate chain that the bear wore around his neck. It magnified his one eye to nearly twice its size. And when he peered at the cubs, they felt as if the reflections of that eye dug into their deepest beings. It was as if he could see to their very souls.

"Follow me," the bear repeated. "And I'll show you cell block four."

Jytte dug her claws into the ice. "We're not going anywhere, unless it's north."

The odd bear looked at them narrowly. For an instant there was a flash in the piece of glass that distorted his eye. "Why do you need to go north?" he asked.

"Why do you want to know?" Jytte said rather boldly.

"We think," Stellan said, "that if we go to the northern hunting grounds, we might find our da."

"Really now?" The bear paused thoughtfully. "I might be able to help you if you follow me."

"Oh!" Jytte exclaimed, her suspicion giving way to excitement.

Stellan hesitated, but Jytte started nudging him forward.

"C'mon, Stellan. He's a bear, not a toothwalker. And he might be able to lead us to Da!"

"Jytte, this is not a hunting ground. It's a jail. Why would our father be in a jail?"

"I have no idea. I don't even know what a jail is. But we'll never know if you don't move."

"I'm not sure this is such a good idea, Jytte."

The bear took a few steps, then glanced back over his shoulder. "Coming? I have an instrument that could help you find your father."

Jytte looked at Stellan as if to say, *See! Nothing to fear. Quit worrying.*

But Stellan was more worried than ever. He had the uncanny feeling that this bear was playing them for fools. But it was too late to convince Jytte to run away, not when she thought this bear could help them find their da. With growing apprehension, Stellan walked slower and slower, lagging behind his sister until he finally stopped short. Jytte turned to him.

"What's wrong?" she hissed.

"I don't know. I just have a feeling. I don't think this is good."

The strange bear turned again. "Are you coming or not?"

"This is very different from the other dens we passed," Stellan whispered. Those dens had offered shelter, respite for creatures. But these dens called cells offered no peace. There were long claw marks along the walls made by enraged bears, and the bars in the openings had been torn out or bent. Whatever living creature had been here — bear or other — had not denned here willingly but had tried to break out. The air seemed to reek of desperation from a long time ago.

The bear stopped short and swung his massive head around. The glass no longer covered his eye, and they could see his face clearly. The cubs tried not to gasp. His face was crisscrossed with black lines, fighting scars that revealed the black skin underneath the fur.

"You call those dens?" he said. "They're shacks. The Others built them. This is a gilly town."

"Gilly town?" Jytte asked. "You mean like ghosts?"

"Yes, like ghosts from when the Others were here."

"You mean there are *gillygaskins* of the Others here?" Stellan asked.

"No, no ghosts of the Others. Not one, I promise you. Just their silly shacks. No decent bear would spend a minute, not a second in them!"

But, thought Stellan, *you don't mind living where decent bears never would.*

The older bear fiddled with the chain a bit. Stellan sensed the bear's mind creaking to life, but what he was thinking was impossible to know. It was as if a scrim of fog ice had formed over the bear's thoughts.

However, behind that scrim, the bear's mind was working feverishly. Uluk Uluk couldn't quite believe his fortune. These cubs, in addition to their natural gifts, had betrayed rare intelligence. It was true that they had no knowledge of the Ice Clock, but they had the imagination to ask the right questions.

The bear nodded toward Stellan. "Are you First or Second?"

"Neither," Stellan replied. For some reason, he was not eager to share his new name with this bear.

"Oh good, so your mother named you before she went off."

How does he know she left us? Stellan wondered.

"We named ourselves," Jytte replied. "I'm Jytte and my brother's name is Stellan."

"You named yourselves?" said the bear. "I'm very impressed."

"What's your name?" Jytte asked.

The bear looked down and shuffled uneasily. It almost seemed as if he had forgotten his own name. "I am Uluk Uluk. Now follow me into the horology laboratory, cell block six."

"I thought we were going to cell block four," Jytte said.

"Changed my mind. Cell block six suits you better."

"And the instrument that will help us find our father?"

"Trust me. To cell block six. Slightly east of north." He paused, then crouched down and peered into both their eyes. "You trust me, don't you, Stellan and Jytte?" The splinter of the rising moon flashed in the glass eyepiece and appeared to fracture his black eye into shards of light. For Jytte, there was no choice. He had an instrument that could lead her to their father.

The cubs, standing upright, reached for each other's paws as they followed the bear called Uluk Uluk. *Heart grit*, Stellan thought. *Heart grit! But do I trust him?*

BEAR
CONTAINMENT
FACILITY

CHAPTER 17

Violation 106

Svenna was at her desk in the Numera, working on her calculations, when she heard Hanne's lumbering gate. The sound was distinctive, as Hanne had somehow lost half of one foot. Svenna started sliding the teeth on her abacus. She mustn't be found moping, as she sensed that Hanne had been asked to spy on her, report any . . . any what? Natural behavior such as missing her cubs? Anything that would distract her from her work at the Ice Clock?

"Ah! Working on the arc calcs, are you?" Hanne asked.

"Yes," Svenna muttered as a meaningless set of numbers swirled in her head. *How long do I have to do this? How long can I stand it?* She derived absolutely no pleasure from finding the correct value, the equations solved.

"I see you're progressing nicely."

"But what am I progressing *toward*?"

Hanne stared at her blankly. "I don't quite understand your meaning."

"How long will my service last? Am I progressing toward a completion?"

"Completion?" The black sheen in Hanne's eyes dulled with a fog of confusion.

"Completion of my service."

"But you do not want to be complete, you want to *advance*."

"So what do I advance to?"

"Well, there are many roles here. Who knows, Master Udo might promote you to a grade two in the Oscillaria. Many would be envious. It took me forever just to get into the Oscillaria." She scratched her head. "I can't even remember how many years I spent on the very lowest level."

A chill mist crept through her. "But my cubs, Hanne!" Hanne looked blank, as if the word hadn't even registered.

"Cubs?" Hanne asked. "Why should you care about cubs when you are working at the clock? We are servants of the Ice Clock. We are members of the Gilraan, the Holy Order of the Timekeepers' Authority. At the rate you're going, you might advance all the way to the Court of Chimes."

Hanne wandered off, leaving Svenna's head swimming. She couldn't do this. She couldn't stay here forever, performing meaningless calculations until she withered away. She cleared her throat. "Preceptor Ragvar, I have a question."

The grizzled older bear grunted from his desk. Svenna took it as consent.

"I want to know how the clock has the power to prevent the next Great Melting. I don't understand this at all. The clock is not a living . . ."

The room fell silent. Preceptor Ragvar gave a sharp snarl and stood up. "How dare you question the power of our sacred clock!" He raised a large bone strung with the immense teeth of a toothwalker and began rattling it.

Two of the Issengards appeared at Svenna's side, yanking her from the ice bench. She could smell the fresh beluga-whale blood on their chests. Normally she would have been salivating at the enticing odor, but her mouth was dry with fear.

One of the bears called out, "Violation number 106 of the Complication Code."

"Oh dear," Hanne mewled. "She's off to solitary, the ice lock."

"Sorry to lose her," Preceptor Ragvar said. "She was turning into an excellent oscillator. Too smart for her own good. But not quite smart enough."

Hanne watched as they hauled Svenna off. She had liked her new denmate. But she should have known from the start — Svenna asked too many questions. She wasn't even sure how one went about such a thing. It had been so long since she had ever even thought of one, let alone actually asked a question, that she had nearly forgotten how.

CHAPTER 18

Cell Block Six

It was a long walk to cell block six, especially because Uluk Uluk moved so slowly.

"Doesn't it seem sort of strange to you, Jytte, that he didn't seem to really know about the northern hunting grounds?" Stellan whispered. "I mean, he's a male bear, you'd think he would know. Then all of a sudden he's talking about this instrument that can help us find north."

"It's not strange at all. Look how skinny he is. I don't think he's been hunting, I mean real hunting, in ages."

"Maybe." Stellan sighed. "He looks pretty old. Old and frail."

As the cubs followed, each wrestling with their anxieties and hopes, Uluk Uluk was having thoughts of his own. These two little cubs could right the wrongs of the past. Wrest the clock from the shameless Timekeepers and their vile beliefs. It was a long shot, of course. And if they failed, it'd mean certain death. But so many cubs had already been sacrificed, what would two more matter if it was for a truly righteous cause? To lie in service of a greater truth, was that really that bad? The truth was that the sheer evilness of the Ice Clock must end. And if only two might die to stop the slaughter of so many, well, so be it.

Uluk Uluk looked back over his shoulder. "Come along, cubs. We're almost there. The moon is rising. A good angle tonight. You'll see it all better."

Jytte gasped as she and Stellan followed Uluk Uluk into cell block six. A soft radiance suffused the darkness. "Is this Ursulana?" Jytte whispered as she tipped back her head in amazement, looking up at the ceiling. "Ursulana with golden stars?"

Dangling from the ceiling were hundreds and hundreds of small metal pieces of varying shape — some were round notched discs, others were coiled springs. There were crescent-shaped pieces that reminded Jytte of the newest or the oldest moons, very polished moons at that. On a high table there were larger pieces of darker metals.

"You think this is our bear heaven, Ursulana, and that these are stars?" Uluk Uluk shook his head in disbelief. "It's not Ursulana. It's my laboratory. Where I do my work."

"What kind of work?" Stellan asked, gazing at the table.

"Building blocks and repairing — and taking apart — all sorts of timepieces." Uluk Uluk paused. "That is my work — time."

"Time is your work?" Jytte turned from the dangling forest of little golden pieces that stirred above her head. The bear's face, with its blackened scars, appeared ghastly in this light.

"I don't like this, Jytte," Stellan whispered. "I think we should leave."

"The instrument, Stellan. With it we might be able to find Da."

Their whispering was interrupted when Uluk Uluk took a step closer and pointed at the shiny objects dangling from the ceiling. "Yes, this is my laboratory. The sounds you hear are caused by the wind stirring the moving parts."

"Moving parts of what?" Jytte asked.

"Of the timepieces as they stir in the wind. I call the parts the innards. As you know from preying on seal, or any animal, there are innards once we tear their bellies open."

"Why do you want to know all this?" Stellan asked.

"I'm curious. Intellectual curiosity. I like to build things. And take them apart. Do you like to build things, cubs?" Although Stellan had asked the question, the old bear focused his attention on Jytte.

"My sister likes to build things. She's an expert in building stuff from snow and ice. She understands how the pieces, the crystals, can lock together," Stellan replied.

Ah! thought Uluk Uluk. *The girl is indeed an ice gazer. Truly gifted!* Yes, these were the cubs he'd been waiting for. Unlike the other poor, foolish cubs who were forced to become Tick Tocks, these two might be able to cause real damage before they succumbed to their grisly fate.

"Would you like to play a game? Not many cubs are good at it, but I know you two will excel."

"We don't have time," Stellan began. "We need to —"

Jytte cut him off. "Yes! We love games. Stellan just knows that I'll beat him. I beat him at everything."

Uluk Uluk chuckled. "This game requires you to work together, as a team. Come with me." He led them back over to his worktable. "I'm going to give you a very sturdy timepiece, and you're going to take it apart. Break it, in fact."

Jytte shot him a questioning look. "How is that a game?"

"Perhaps 'challenge' is a better word. Do you think you're up to it?"

Jytte narrowed her eyes as she surveyed the timepiece. "I think so."

"Now let me ask you one very important thing. Do you know what makes a timepiece break?" Both cubs shook their heads. "Friction," said Uluk Uluk.

"What's friction?" Stellan asked.

"Resistance, struggle, opposition."

"A fight?" Jytte asked.

"Not exactly. To work properly, timepieces must have absolutely no friction. No resistance for all the innards — the small parts — to move. One could damage the timepiece if resistance were introduced. Say, grit, or small crystals of granite. The energy would not be transferred correctly. And eventually the clock would stop." He sighed. "Yes, it would stop completely."

Uluk Uluk placed a timepiece on a slab in front of them facedown. With a flick of a claw tip he popped off the back. The cubs' eyes widened as they peered into a cluster of springs and small discs with interlocking teeth. Sparkling jewels were nested in the center of each disc. There was a chorus of little clicks. Jytte tipped her head and listened. The sound reminded her of the infinitesimally small clicks she heard during the crackling moons, when the tiniest splits formed in the hardest ice.

Uluk Uluk clapped his paws together. "Ready? I'm going to time you to see how long you take to stop this timepiece . . . okay . . . go!"

Stellan fixed his eyes on the disc with the teeth, the source of sounds. He felt a shiver run down his spine as a strange image formed in his head — the disc *eating* something. But eating what? Time? In his mind's eye, he saw those teeth dripping with blood.

A slender forked piece swung to and fro interlocking with each tooth. Jam that and the terrible toothed disc would stop.

Jytte was clearly thinking the same thing. Before Stellan could move, she picked up a grain of grit from the table and dropped it just between the forked piece and the disc. Instantly the clicks were silenced. The movement stopped. Stellan let out a long sigh of relief as the gruesome images in his head faded. The clock was jammed.

"We did it!" Jytte exclaimed.

"Well done, cubs," Uluk Uluk said. He was clearly pleased, but there was a note of something else in his voice, something that made Stellan uneasy. "Now you know what to do if you ever need to stop a timepiece."

"Why would we ever need to do that?" Stellan asked, ignoring Jytte's eye roll.

Uluk Uluk stared at Stellan. "You may find yourself facing challenges you never imagined, cub. All I can tell you is to trust those instincts of yours. They'll serve you well."

"All we care about right now is finding our father," Stellan said stiffly.

"Of course, of course!" Uluk Uluk went and fetched something that hung in a corner of the cell. "Now, cubs, pay attention. This instrument is what I call a red band timepiece. In the time of the Others, it was called a compass watch. It can show you the direction you are traveling in relation to the sun. You know that during the Winter Ice Moons when the sun almost rises there is just a stain of red, a red shadow on the horizon. The same thing happens when it sets in the west." The cubs nodded. "Well, with this timepiece, you move the hands to the exact position of that stain. It will help you keep directly north, if indeed you know where east and west is from the stain.

"Come, cubs, let's go outside and try it. The red band should soon be showing in the east. And the east is where the sun rises. You shall want to bear just east of north. You'll know when you are closing in on the hunting grounds as the ice becomes *klarken*." He shot a glance at Jytte whose ears pricked up.

"Klarken?"

"Yes, hunters seek it. It's almost transparent. It's a solid precipitation, a reverse vaporization process that forms the ice far in the north when large drops of water freeze during a fog. Very good for hunters. They can almost see through the ice to the seals swimming below. It's why they go there to those far northern reaches. Best hunting anywhere. And then of course you'll start to see the formation of the Schrynn Gar clouds that come from the east. Start heading a bit more east when you see those clouds."

"Why?" Jytte asked.

"It's the true course to the hunting grounds."

Uluk Uluk shoved aside the guilt forming in his gut. Yes, if they followed his directions, the Roguers would find them, but if the cubs were as clever as they seemed, they might be able to jam the clock before they were forced onto the wheel with the other Tick Tocks.

Stellan caught fragments of this thought, but there were too many words he did not know — *Tick Tocks?* And what was a *wheel?*

They left cell block six by climbing through an opening with no bars. Uluk Uluk moved stiffly as he hoisted his front leg over the ledge. The snow was knee deep on the cubs but ankle deep for Uluk Uluk. It had grown darker and the blackness seemed to shudder around them.

"Now, you see this third hand?" Uluk Uluk continued his demonstration. "This hand we'll set in the direction you want to go. This other hand is for the red band that you set each morning and evening when the stain appears on the horizon."

Jytte's eyes glimmered with anticipation.

"North," Jytte whispered as if the word was magical. "North to the hunting grounds."

"Exactly! North to the best hunting grounds," Uluk Uluk said. The lie slipped off his blue tongue so easily. He just needed to make sure the cubs ended exactly where he wanted them to go: Oddsvall, in the Ublunkyn region near the Ice Cap. "You'll know you're drawing close when you reach an island archipelago. The islands sit in the Oddsvall lead — a very wide lead that serves as a passageway for whales. You must watch carefully in this region for the *blyndspryee.*"

"What's a blyndspryee?" Stellan asked.

"It is a sudden violent storm with a blinding wind that can arise within the blink of an eye. You must grasp each other, for if you get separated, you might never find each other again. Cubs perish in blyndspryees. It was said that the bones of one cub were once found across the Schrynn Gar gap."

Stellan stepped forward, extending his paw to take the timepiece. "Thank you, sir. I think this will help us with our mission. Now we must be on our way."

"I would advise that you stay through this night until the next. Good to be rested."

"I think we really should be leaving."

"On an empty stomach? I have some well-aged caribou."

"Boo boo meat!" Jytte clapped her paws.

"We're not hungry," Stellan lied. Oh how he wished his sister would just shut up.

"C'mon, now. I smell the halibut on you, but boo boo, as you call it, Jytte, now there's a meat that sticks to your ribs."

"Yes, let's stay, Stellan."

Uluk Uluk didn't wait for him to respond. "Follow me, cubs, and I'll share my boo boo with you."

"Hey, that rhymes!" Jytte said merrily. "Share my boo boo with you."

Urskadamus! Stellan thought. This sister would be the death of him. But then again, this same sister had saved his life.

He looked at Jytte. She was too thin. They needed the meat. Stellan knew they had to stay.

And so, as the deepening blackness of the night and the shadows of his own fears shuddered around Stellan, he followed silently.

CHAPTER 19

Murmurs of the Gillygaskins

It was a small cell. Hardly big enough to turn around in. It was made of a rough kind of ice that was not the least bit comfortable for sleeping, but Svenna supposed that was the point. And there were no portals through which to view the clock, or the sky. She didn't miss the clock. But she missed the sky. There was one unexpected benefit — a gift, really, a blessing of sorts from Great Ursus. She had time now to think about her cubs. The endless numbers of the equations were beginning to release their claws from her mind. She would no longer gasp for memories like a dying creature for air.

Svenna raised a paw and scratched out some calculations — not about the clock. No, she was figuring out how long she had been in ice lock. Four days and thirteen hours. She could not glimpse the clock from ice lock, but she diligently kept track of the quarter-hour chimes and the louder ones that rang every hour.

She heard the heavy tread of the jailer come down the corridor and quickly began to erase her claw calculations from the ice floor. She bent over and licked off the last scratchings with her tongue. An odd taste suddenly filled her mouth.

Blood!

"Numerator Svenna," the guard's voice called out.

Quickly she sat up, placing her bottom squarely on the ice patch she had been licking.

"Ah, there you are." The guard held a quill and piece of sealscap parchment in one paw, an abacus in the other. He set down the abacus. "Because of your good behavior these past four days, thirteen hours, fifty-two minutes, and" — he lifted a massive paw as he silently counted his claw tips — "and three seconds, you will be permitted to have quill and parchment to resume your calculations for the Oscillaria. Here is the log. And I shall bring a work clock for pendulum arc measurements."

Svenna, with the taste of blood still in her mouth, stared at him. "Would tomorrow evening at this hour be sufficient?"

"You mean at eighteen hundred hours, twenty-four minutes, and thirty-five seconds?"

She blinked. "Yes, that's what I meant."

The guard slid the parchment and quill through the slot to her. He looked directly at her. "Yes, that is sufficient. But I'd advise you not to ask any more foolish questions."

As soon as she was certain he was gone, she was on her paws and knees examining the red stain. She determined that it was not fresh blood but old blood. She took another lick. "Oh no!" she groaned, feeling a stab to her heart. Svenna knew beyond a doubt that this was the blood of a cub, possibly a still-nursing cub. She could almost taste the milky sweetness. What had happened to its mother? Was she not able to make a deal — a service swap so her cub could live free?

Svenna picked up the quill and looked at it. It was a mottled dusky gray with touches of brownish red and black, similar to the coloring but not the pattern of a barred owl. "Ah, must be a whiskered screech — like Lyze of Kiel. Wonder what that old sage of an owl, so long dead, would think of all this?" she murmured to herself. Then she worked on the calcs.

She heard twelve bells and decided to stop. She was suddenly very tired. As soon as she lay down, she fell into a deep slumber. She felt herself being pulled away. Far away from the horrid clock to another world, a world of infinite sky and swirling stars. A feather drifted by on the trailing edge of a breeze. Then ahead she saw the owl flying. It looked back. One eye was clenched in a perpetual squint. One foot missing a talon, a deep gouge in his beak. He was as scarred as an old fighting bear. It could be only one bird — Lyze of Kiel, or Ezylryb, as he had been called at the Great Tree of Ga'Hoole. Why had he flown into her dreams? But were these dreams? They seemed so real. The owl dissolved in a thickening fog.

She heard a soft chuffing sound, the kind cubs made when demanding to nurse. She opened her eyes wide. In the corner of her cell, a very tiny cub was hunched over, weeping.

Svenna walked toward it. "Why are you weeping, cub?" she asked gently, wondering how the cub got into her cell.

The cub shook its head and buried its chin deep in the fur of its tiny chest, as if ashamed of something.

"Now, what is it, dear? You can tell me. Are you hungry?" The cub shook its head. Not hungry. That was good, because the last of her milk had dried up.

"So can you tell me why you are crying, little one?"

"I . . . I have . . . no shadow!" the cub sobbed.

"No shadow? But of course not. There is no light in here. To have a shadow in a dark place, you need light."

The cub shook his head. "No. That's not why. I would not have a shadow on the brightest moonlit night." He tucked his head deeper into his chest fur.

"Tell me, little one, why would you not have a shadow on the brightest moonlit night?"

"Because I'm not alive." He paused. "I'm a gillygaskin."

Svenna inhaled sharply. "A ghost?"

"A gillygaskin." He raised his head. She gasped. His muzzle was stained in blood.

Then it dawned on Svenna. "You're a Tick Tock!"

"I was until I died."

Oh, Ursus, thought Svenna, *let my cubs be far, far from here.*

CHAPTER 20

"I Don't Want to Be a Tick Tock!"

Stellan and Jytte had left Uluk Uluk the previous evening, just before the red band started to melt into the darkness of the night. They were now traveling through a sparse wood. Jytte looked down at the timepiece. "We are at four hours and thirty-five minutes and ten seconds from our starting point. So we are exactly on the track that Uluk Uluk set for us."

"That's what concerns me," Stellan replied in a worried voice.

"What do you mean?"

"I mean, maybe he doesn't want us to find our father or the hunting grounds, Jytte."

"Why would you ever say that? Of course he does."

There was no *of course* about it in Stellan's mind. It seemed odd that this strange bear would take such an interest in them.

"You worry too much, Stellan. Uluk Uluk wants to help us! He must know how to get to the hunting grounds. He must have hunted there once."

"Once! And that had to be a long time ago. You saw how skinny he was. You said it yourself. Things could have changed."

"You're always so suspicious, Stellan. You don't trust anyone."

"No, you're wrong. I just don't trust Uluk Uluk," Stellan replied calmly.

Jytte clenched her teeth. She was fuming inside. But they had promised each other that night when Lago left that they would not fight again. Still, not fighting was harder sometimes than fighting. They walked on in icy silence.

They were looking for a river that Uluk Uluk promised would not be frozen but would have good fish to eat. The cubs were hungry. The caribou had not stuck to their ribs as Uluk Uluk had promised. But nothing could squelch Jytte's excitement as they headed north to find their father. At least ten times since they had left Uluk Uluk, she had burst out gleefully, "We're really on our way. On our way north!" And every time she said these words, Stellan thought, *Something is wrong. We should not have trusted that bear.*

They were in a short wood, which meant a forest with very small trees because they were so far above the tree line. The cubs had often visited such forests in the summertime when the ice receded. But the short wood looked very different in the winter moons. Snow had transformed the landscape. The trees were so stubby that they disappeared under huge drifts of snow, and so did the streams and rivers. Stellan's stomach growled loudly. Jytte sighed. She felt similar rumblings in her own stomach.

"You know it's only going to get worse," Stellan said.

"Why?"

"As we get bigger, our stomachs will get bigger. We'll have to eat more, or else . . ."

"Or else what?" Jytte asked irritably.

"Or else our pelts will hang off us like Uluk Uluk's and puddle around our feet."

"Thank you, Stellan, for reminding me how terrible we'll look soon."

"Don't get cranky, Jytte."

"Being hungry makes me cranky, and your being such a wet pelt makes me even crankier."

"Well, Jytte, being hungry makes some bears dead. It's called starving to death."

Jytte felt her remaining patience with her brother begin to shred. If it wasn't his hind paw and ruddering problems, it was something else. It was always something with him! He seemed to live to worry. "Urskadamus!"

"You swore, Jytte! What would Mum think?"

"Mum isn't here to think. She left us. Remember? She left us to go off to look for that . . . that miserable place."

"Miserable place? It's the Den of Forever Frost. The place of noble and valiant bears. Heroes." Tears began to leak from Stellan's eyes.

"I don't want a mum or a da that's a hero. I just want a plain mum and da." Jytte stomped her foot. They heard a crack. "Eeeyii!" she screamed. She pulled her foot up. It was drenched. "This is the river, Stellan. We've found the river!"

"That's a river?" Stellan said, looking down. "Well . . . more of a creek than a river," he muttered.

"So you're saying this isn't a river, Stellan? Look at this. I'm wet up to my knee. Do I have to *drown* in it to prove that this is the river Uluk Uluk was talking about? Oh, I forgot you wouldn't even be able to save me. Not with your useless hind paws and ruddering!"

Stellan winced. "That was nasty, Jytte."

"Sorry," Jytte mumbled, realizing she'd gone too far.

In truth it was a creek tucked snugly under billows of snow. The ice wasn't that thick, and underneath they found barely moving winter-sleep fish. The fish were easy to catch, and the cubs ate until finally Jytte announced, "One more fish and I'll grow scales."

Suddenly, they heard a noise, a raw voice carried by the wind.

"What is that?" Stellan whispered.

"Shhh! It's coming this way." They listened a few more seconds. It was the familiar snuffy little whines of distress. The words, garbled at first, became clearer.

"I don't want to be a Tick Tock . . . I don't want to be . . ." The words *Tick Tock* scratched at the back of Jytte's mind. She had heard those words before, but where?

"It's a cub, Jytte," Stellan said anxiously. "It's in trouble."

A figure staggered toward them in the milky light of a half-moon.

"Third!" Stellan exclaimed.

"It can't be." Jytte's voice was thick with wonder.

"But it is!" Stellan bounded over to the little fellow and crouched down. "Climb up, Third. Climb up on my back. I'll carry you over to some fish."

The scrawny cub tried to climb up but slipped off with a low moan.

"Here, Third," Jytte said. "I'll help you up onto Stellan's back." She had forgotten how small young cubs were, and Third was even smaller.

Jytte began stripping off the flesh of the leftover fish and feeding him small bits.

"Open your mouth, Third, that's it. Yeah, I know, different from Mum's milk."

"I have a feeling he hasn't had much of Mum's milk lately," Stellan said.

Third looked at them, blinking, while he swallowed.

In between bites he kept repeating, "No . . . no Tick Tock . . . I don't want to be a Tick Tock."

Gradually, the foggy glaze that filled his eyes began to clear.

Stellan leaned in closer. "Third, you know us, don't you? We were Fourth and Fifth."

"No," he said quietly. "You were First and Second." He paused. "No Tick Tock."

A frightened looked came into his eyes, and the tiny cub fell back into a faint.

"Oh no, what have I done?" Jytte gasped.

"He's not dead. Don't worry." Stellan began rubbing snow in the cub's face. "I think we have to get out onto the sea ice again. This little fellow needs blubber. Seal blubber. He's starving to death. I bet Taaka kicked him out of the den."

Jytte had a more dreadful thought, which she did not say out loud, but once again Stellan read her mind.

"Jytte, you think that Taaka was going to eat this cub?" he asked quietly.

"Kill him and feed him to the other two," Jytte muttered.

"Great Ursus, a mother could do this?" Stellan said, stunned.

"Taaka could." They both looked at the tiny scrap of a cub and wondered how Third had ever made his way so far.

As gently as possible, Stellan lifted the little cub to his shoulder, and he and his sister headed north and two points east to the Frozen Sea.

They were glad to be back on the ice. Yet it was with great trepidation that they approached the first breathing hole that they found.

Third slipped from Stellan's back. They had no fear that he would make any noise. He had been virtually mute since he had fainted — not a single word about Tick Tocks, whatever they were. Nor had there been any whimpering. Jytte and Stellan flattened themselves against the ice and were perfectly still. This time they had worked it out. Only one of them would grab for the surfacing seal. They would not risk getting their paws stuck again. It was decided Stellan would smack the seal after Jytte grabbed it.

"Do I smack first and then lift it from the hole? Or lift and then smack when it's out of the hole?" Stellan asked. "I can't remember how Mum did it."

"Lift . . . smack." But it was not Jytte who answered. It was Third. They turned to him in amazement. How would he know? He was nearly a year younger and had most likely not yet been out on the ice with his mum.

"How do you know that?" Jytte asked.

The little cub shrugged. He barely spoke more than a few words at a time.

Perhaps he didn't know many. It was hard to imagine Third having conversations with his brutish bigger brother and sister. And Stellan seriously doubted Taaka would ever tell her cubs stories as their mum had.

"So, you got that, Jytte? You lift and I smack?" Stellan asked.

"Got it." Within seconds, she heard a stirring under the ice. She could almost catch the seal's scent. *Great Ursus*, she thought, *don't make this seal Jameson*. But she couldn't take time to really look. She had to act quickly. The top of the seal's head broke through the water. Jytte clawed its neck and hauled it from the hole. There was a resounding slap, then the head lolled to one side.

"Well done, Stellan!" Jytte shouted.

But before they could take their first bite, they heard a whimper behind them. "What's the matter, little fellow?" Stellan turned around to look at Third, and his blood turned to ice.

A large black wolf melted out of the night. A strange green fire glowed in his eyes, and his fangs glistened in the moonlight. His hackles were raised.

"Oh no!" Jytte whispered, feeling her own guard hairs stiffen as a sickish feeling invaded her. He was a huge wolf.

Fear engulfed Stellan. His heart was thundering in his chest. He felt the tiny cub trembling against his leg. He reached out and dragged Third back, shoving him behind them. But the wolf kept advancing, swinging his head menacingly from side to side. In the moonlight the wolf's shadow spread out on the ice as if claiming the vast frozen sea. Stellan thought he could read the creature's thoughts. *Mine, mine . . . all this is mine.* A scent rolled off it. Not the wolf's scent but that of his latest kill — a cub!

The distance between them was shrinking. Stellan could see the wolf's shoulder muscles begin to bunch beneath the fur, readying to charge. With each second Stellan felt a suffocating desperation. *I must breathe, breathe and think, if we are to survive.*

The wolf stopped short, a crazed look in his eyes. Stellan could feel the beast's hunger, hunger for them. He let out a harsh growl, fierce and commanding. "Submit! Submit!" Stellan understood this strange language immediately. The wolf's tail was stiff and straight out.

Stellan recalled their mum saying that wolves, though much smaller than bears, made up for it with their cunning. *They might be small, but they know exactly how to slice the life-pumping artery. There's always a lot of blood when a wolf kills.*

When a wolf kills. The words echoed in both the cubs' minds. They felt each other's fear, fear for themselves and fear for little Third. Within seconds they could be destroyed. Jytte imagined the rip of his fangs in her own flesh. She wanted to flee, but that was unthinkable. She would rather die than flee. Jytte dug her claws into the ice. She would not see her brother hurt. She must be cunning, cunning as a wolf. She looked down at the dead seal and pushed it toward the stalking wolf, but slightly to the side.

"He wants both," Stellan whispered to Jytte.

"Both?"

"The seal and Third. He's expecting us to hand over Third."

"No!" Jytte let out a low growl and, without thinking, rushed toward the wolf.

"Jytte!" Stellan shrieked. He saw blood fly through the air as Jytte skidded across the ice. The wolf charged after her, but she dodged and seemed to vanish into thin air. Stellan sensed she was behind a pile of old jumble ice, but the wolf seemed mystified. He stood there quivering, trying to catch Jytte's scent. He swung his head back toward Stellan. *He's confused*, Stellan thought. *He doesn't want to turn his back on me to look for Jytte.*

Behind the jumble ice, Jytte was panting, trying to catch her breath, when something truly extraordinary occured in her mind. For the first time in her life, she knew exactly what Stellan was thinking. Not just sensed. She could hear his thoughts. *Decoy!* she heard.

Stellan inhaled sharply as he felt his sister wandering through his thoughts. *Decoy!* he thought again. *We need a decoy.*

The wolf kept turning his head to look for Jytte, who was still crouched behind the mass of jumble-ice fragments. The ice was heavy, and the slabs appeared immovable. But she saw a telltale crack in one of the foundation pieces. If she clawed that, it just might make the entire mound crash. And that would be a distraction! She wedged a claw into the crack. There was a creak, then a loud crack!

The guard hairs on the wolf bristled. He turned his head.

Now! The neck, Stellan! The neck! Jytte willed. In that moment Stellan forgot his fear. A hot fury swelled within him like a thunderbolt, and he charged. For the wolf, Stellan was a blur on the periphery of his sight. But the wolf's neck presented the perfect target. Stellan leaped and sank his teeth in his neck. Blood spurted into air that was spangled with frost crystals. The wolf landed on the ice with a bone-shaking thud, then lay still. He was dead, his eyes flung open as if he couldn't quite believe what had just happened to him. Jytte limped out from behind the wreckage of ice.

"You're hurt, sister."

"Not really." She let out a ragged breath. "He caught me with his claws, not his fangs. Between your haunch and my shoulder, we are going to be as crisscrossed with fighting scars as Uluk Uluk's face."

It was a necessary kill, but it was not one to celebrate. The wolf was stealing their prey. They did what had to be done. Jytte and Stellan looked into each other's eyes. A realization threaded through them: *We have no one. We take care of these things ourselves now.*

The three cubs turned their backs on the wolf and began to tear at the seal. With each bite, Third gained strength. Indeed, he almost appeared to grow fatter before their eyes. Jytte and

Stellan were both immensely curious about Third. What had Taaka done to him? How had he come all this way? They felt, however, that such questions had to wait until Third was stronger.

They had not been feasting long when they spotted crows, blacker than the night, circling above the carcass. One swooped down and began sniffing around the wolf's body. Another landed and started clawing at the large gash in the wolf's neck.

"It's okay," Jytte said. "I don't think they're interested in our seal."

"We really did it." Stellan stared at the seal in awe. "Remember our mouse days?"

"Don't remind me," Jytte replied. "I suppose we'll know we're real hunters when we're tailed by a Nunquivik fox instead of crows."

"You are a real hunter, Jytte." Stellan looked up. A blob of blubber hung from the corner of his mouth. "You hooked that seal right in the neck and hauled it up."

She tucked her chin and felt a warm thrill run through her. *My brother thinks I'm a real hunter!* "Thanks, Stellan."

A strong wind suddenly swept down on them.

"We better find an ice snug for the night. The *ukhar* is starting to blow. I feel its fangs," Stellan said. The ukhar winds, named for their sharp, slicing edges, were particularly heavy during the Second Seal Moon.

Stellan stood on his hind legs with Third upon his shoulders. *My, he has grown*, thought Jytte regarding her brother. She wondered if she had grown as tall. She stood up as well and joined him in scanning the horizon. The red band was just showing. She checked the timepiece. Yes, they were still on track with the course Uluk Uluk had set. The pointer for true north always lined up with Nevermoves, and they would keep two points to the east of it, as Uluk Uluk had told them.

The ice on the sea was changing. It was different from when they had first gone on it after finding Third. But it was not yet the klarken ice.

"Over there, a snug!" Third said, pointing with his small paw toward a pressure ridge. Pressure ridges always offered good wind protection.

Stellan tipped his head up. "Good work, Third." He gave the cub's leg an affectionate pat.

Third beamed with pride. That simple little pat on his leg was as good as the taste of blubber. "I'll tell you my story when we find shelter. I promise." Words seemed to be coming more easily to him now. "But can you tell me where are you going? What are you looking for? Your mum? I know some mums are good."

Stellan sighed wistfully. "Our mum was very good. But we think it might be easier to find our father."

"Our da," Jytte said. "He's in the northern hunting grounds. That's why we look for Nevermoves."

"Nevermoves?" Third asked.

"The star that points north. Our mother showed it to us."

"Your mother showed you the stars?" Third's voice was filled with wonder.

"Yes," Jytte said. "And pointed out the ones she and our da were named for."

"Goodness!" Third exclaimed softly.

As the three cubs walked off from their kill site, the crows lifted their heads from the carcass. Their beaks were bloody. The largest of the crows nodded to the other three. They set off in the opposite direction of the cubs and rose, flapping, like rags of darkness in the sky.

CHAPTER 21

The Powers of Third

Snow had collected on the downwind side of a pressure ridge, sculpting the edge into waves. The Nevermoves star was in the place it should be, and the twin stars Jytte and Stellan were scampering off just ahead of the star called Svree. With the reappearance of these stars, and with the additional help of the red band timepiece, the cubs knew they were going in the right direction.

They had hauled the seal to a snug beneath the pressure ridge where they had dug out the snug even deeper. It was cozy and protected them well. As they settled down, their bellies full, they were ready to hear Third's story.

Jytte looked at Third, tucked in the crook of Stellan's arm. He was so tiny. How had he survived long enough to get to that place near the river where they had found him?

"So she kicked you out of the den?"

Third hesitated for several seconds before nodding. "But it wasn't just about milk. Or fighting for my share." He paused, tears brimming in his eyes. "She yelled a lot . . . A lot."

"At you?" Stellan asked.

"Yes."

"Why?"

"She was scared of me."

Stellan stared at Third with confusion. "What? Why?" How could Taaka be frightened of this little cub? The weakest of all her cubs? Was there something that he and Jytte were missing?

"Scared of you? But you're so tiny and powerless," Jytte added.

There was another long pause. It seemed that the words Third was trying to summon were falling away before they reached his mouth. "I'm not exactly powerless. I do have certain powers."

"You do?" Stellan said.

"I think Mum knew it before I did. See, I have these dreams at night — strange, scary dreams." The words now came out of Third in a rush. "I guess I would mostly mumble, but sometimes I'd cry out. Mum would just shove me out of the den, and my dreaming became even stronger. I realized that the dreams that were the scariest weren't *my* dreams at all but my mum's."

"Wait," Stellan said. A sudden queasiness seized him, as if he had eaten rotten blubber. "You could see your mum's dreams?"

"It's hard to understand, but it was as if I was inside my mum's head. And I'll tell you, it's an evil country. I can't call her mum anymore. Inside Taaka's head . . . she's not right."

He can't call her mum! Stellan thought. How terrible for a little cub to even have to say this, let alone have to wander through the evilness of his mother's twisted mind.

"It took me a while to understand that the dreams weren't mine but hers. It was where I learned the words 'Tick Tocks.'"

"What did you see in her dreams?" Jytte asked.

"I saw blood and fur on something called a wheel — a wheel that had teeth."

Stellan began to tremble, but said nothing.

"I saw something that looks a bit like this." Third reached out and touched the red band timepiece suspended on the chain hanging from Jytte's neck. She jerked back. "But the one I saw was huge!"

"And what about the Tick Tocks?" Stellan asked.

"I'm still not sure. But I know it means something terrible, and that I was going to become one. That was Taaka's plan. I heard her talking to my brother."

"What did she say?" Stellan asked.

"She said that I was a freakish little thing and to stay away from me when we were allowed to play outside in the snow. She said my brother would never win a game with me because I have something she called 'second sight.' I think she was talking about the dreams."

"But how did you know that you had to leave?" Stellan asked gently, trying to hide his growing horror.

"I had had a dream the night before. It was truly my dream this time. Two huge bears came and carried me off. All jolly, you know, telling me, 'You'll like being a Tick Tock. Tick Tocks will become your best friends.' Then, suddenly, I was in a terrifying place . . . There was this enormous tower made of ice, and I don't know how to describe it, except to say . . ." Third's eyes rested again on the red band timepiece. "I could see right through it, to its very beating heart, and I saw these little cubs walking on the wheel I just told you about, with the teeth. If the cubs missed a step, it devoured them. And I think they are what's called a Tick Tock."

"So you left?" Stellan said.

"As fast as I could."

"But how did you ever find us?" Jytte asked.

"Good dreams, I think. I dreamed of you two and warm, cozy things. I never thought I could really find you." Third paused. "I suppose it's all because of good dreams and good luck."

"Where did the luck come in?" Jytte asked.

"I stumbled onto some jumble ice. That's where I fell asleep the first night. And then I felt this huge jolt that woke me up. The jumble ice had been torn apart and I was floating. The current was rapid. I didn't have much choice. I couldn't jump off. I don't know how to swim. So I stuck with it. I'm not sure how long."

"What did you eat?" Stellan asked.

"A bird accidentally dropped a fish. I ate that. That was all I had until the fish you gave me. Eventually this piece of jumble ice bumped up on a shore. And I had just enough energy to start walking. And . . . and here I am."

Jytte touched the red band timepiece with her paw and felt a tremor pass through her. "It's as if you have a compass watch in your head."

"Maybe," Third replied softly. "Maybe."

Uluk Uluk spotted the tattered wings of the crows as the red band stained the horizon. The crows were the messenger birds of choice in Nunquivik. Before Uluk Uluk had become a hermit in Winston, he had preferred blackpoll warblers. Incredible flyers and navigators, these warblers outstripped the skills of the best navigators of all — the Nunquivik foxes. But the warblers had flown south and would not be returning until the Dying Ice Moons. Uluk Uluk had sent these crows to make sure that the cubs were on a direct track for the Ublunkyn and the Ice Clock.

The crows settled patiently a few feet away, perched on a trough.

"So?" Uluk Uluk said as he picked up a timepiece and began fiddling with it.

The largest crow stepped off the trough and hopped up to the bear. Uluk Uluk felt the eight dark pairs of beady eyes focused on his paws as he tinkered with a spring he had just extracted from the balance wheel.

"They stick to the route north and just east of Nevermoves," the biggest crow cawed. The sound was scratchy, scratchy as a rusty ratchet. He always wanted to oil these crows when they opened their beaks.

Another crow cawed, "Tell him about the third cub."

"Third cub?" Uluk Uluk repeated. "What's this?"

"They picked up another cub."

Uluk Uluk's eyes opened wide. "You don't say?"

"I do say!" The crow's voice scraped the air. "Aren't you going to pay us extra?" the crow asked, eyeing the spring.

"This will do you no good," Uluk Uluk replied. "You wouldn't know what to do with it."

"Are you insulting us?" asked the crow who perched next to the big one.

"No, not at all. I'll find a finer piece of wire for your anting."

The crows adored wire for poking in holes and picking out insects. The creatures would eat just about anything — which reminded Uluk Uluk of one of their more gruesome practices — picking out the eyes of newborn foxes. They loved kits' eyes as much as voles. "No eye picking with the wire, though. Understand."

"Wouldn't dream of it!" the big crow said.

Liar, Uluk Uluk thought. But then again, he was a liar. The biggest liar of them all.

CHAPTER 22

Of Gillygaskins and Other Horrors

"You're a Tick Tock," Svenna whispered to the small cub huddled in the corner of her ice lock cell. Even whispered, the words seemed to scald the air.

The gauzy little bundle nodded.

"And you want your shadow back?" Again the cub nodded. "I don't quite understand. If you get your shadow back, does that mean you will live again?"

"I don't think so."

"Then why would you want your shadow back?"

"We all want them back."

"All?" This stunned Svenna. Were there more cubs like this?

"Yes, there are . . . well, I can't count that high. You see, we can only count to fifteen."

"Why is that?"

"That is how many teeth there are on the escapement wheel."

"Is that what you were doing, trying to escape?"

"Oh no! There's no escape. Only terrible injuries." The gillygaskin held up one forearm. There was no paw.

"If I'd survived, I would have been PIF."

"PIF? What's that?"

"Paid in full."

"But what is paid in full?"

"My tribute payment. I would be released from the wheel."

Svenna felt dread rising inside her. It took all the courage she could muster to ask the next question. "What exactly is the wheel?"

"The escapement wheel. It is where we bleed and die. Our tribute. The tribute of the Tick Tocks."

Svenna staggered a bit. *Great Ursus!* she thought. *What has become of our world? Our once noble bear world?*

"But what are you paying tribute for?"

"The Grand Patek sacrifices us to the clock. That's what prevents another Great Melting. The clock protects us bears, but it demands tribute."

Svenna's head swirled as a wave of nausea crashed over her. This was absolute insanity. But what did any of these bears know about honor?

"And had you survived the wheel, what would do afterward?"

"Who knows? Maybe be a low-level numerator."

Hanne! Svenna thought. Hanne and her half paw.

"So you aren't . . . dead? "

"We are caught between earth and Ursulana. We are *quivik*. Not alive, yet not quite dead. We don't have names. I mean, not real names like the ones our mums might have given us."

"What do you call yourself, little one?"

"Juuls."

"That's a lovely name."

"Still, even with names, no one knows us in Ursulana, the den in the sky where the spirits of bears go when they die. We are nothing. That is the other number you learn as a gillygaskin — zero."

"You are not zero," Svenna said forcefully. "I cannot bring your life back, but I can try, try my hardest, Juuls, to get you to Ursulana. You won't suffer anymore. You'll be able to play."

"Play? What's play?"

The words chilled Svenna to the bone. A cub who did not know about play? How freakish!

"Play is . . . is to roll in the snowdrifts, or slip down an ice slide, or dance under the lights of the ahalikki."

"The ahalikki?"

"You don't know about the beautiful colored lights of the ahalikki that fan through the skies like rippling rainbows?"

Suddenly they heard the footsteps of a guard. "How are you coming with those calcs, madam? Need more time?"

"Uh . . . perhaps," Svenna said. The guard seemed not to see the gillygaskin. He was looking straight at the corner where Svenna's parchment and quill were, right next to the cub's pawless forearm. She didn't understand it. The cub opened his mouth slightly and closed his eyes halfway. He was smiling. Yes, just the way little cubs often expressed happiness, and she could hear little squeaks coming from him too. She felt a twinge in her heart. She would do whatever it took to help this cub and the others.

In a place that was neither here nor there, in a place called quivik, a place of vapor swirling with the scented steam of the fire goblets, hundreds of little gillygaskins seemed to drift. Some lacked paws or feet, arms or legs. One poor soul lacked a head, or rather its head hovered just about its shoulders.

"It worked!" the gillygaskin replied, still smiling.

"You mean the guard didn't see you?"

"No. But she did. The bear called Svenna did!"

"Then she can help us! You'll go back?"

"I'll try. But I'm not sure how much longer she'll be in ice lock, and when she is out, well, you know her denmate is that she-bear Hanne who lost half her foot as a cub on the wheel and nearly died. It could be a problem. Hanne might have a sense about gillygaskins."

"Oh, I think that's just an old gilly tale," said the nearly headless one.

"Perhaps, but I'll go back. Do you know what she said?"

"What, Juuls?"

"She said, 'You are not zero. I cannot bring your life back, but I can try, try my hardest, to get you to Ursulana . . . you'll be able to play . . .'"

"Play?" The word hummed through the vapors. "What do you think that is?" the other gillys murmured.

"I have no idea. But if she can get us to Ursulana . . ." Juuls's voice melted into a deep sigh.

CHAPTER 23

The Belong

The cubs traveled on. It was not easy. There were days when the sky thickened with blizzards or fog and they lost track of the stars. But Jytte's ice gazing had sharpened and she continued noting the changes.

The going was slow, as Stellan's haunch ached from the toothwalker's slashing tusk. And although Jytte had thought the wolf fangs had just gone skin deep, the claw must have grazed a muscle. They were both limping. In Jytte's mind, the journey had been divided into two parts: before the wolf and after the wolf. And in Stellan's mind, there was before the toothwalker and after the toothwalker. Neither cub ever complained, even though Stellan, in his own odd way, felt Jytte's pain in addition to his own. Each wince was like a flinch in his brain.

They must have made some progress north, for it did seem like new country here. There was no open water, no inlets in sight. It was all ice — ice sometimes twisted into strange forms and figures. Some of the ice was crystal clear, and when the moonlight struck it, the shaft of light would break into different colors.

Third stopped abruptly, then stepped into a puddle of violet light. Next he placed his other foot in a puddle of blue light. "Look at this!" he cried with delight. Stellan began moving slowly through the radiant light puddles. "Caught in a rainbow!" he exclaimed.

"It's so boring being white," Jytte said. "Imagine if we could change our colors every day!" Jytte peered deeply into a green patch of ice. She suddenly had a staggering thought. Could this be klarken ice? The ice that Uluk Uluk had told them about? That would be the sure sign that they were entering the richest hunting grounds on earth. Had they actually made it to the northern hunting grounds? A flash of movement caught her eye. She glanced down and saw a seal swimming beneath the ice. Jytte gave a yelp, and, forgetting her pain, she bounced up on her paws and turned a somersault.

"What is it?" Stellan asked, alarmed.

"We're here! Or almost."

"How do you know?"

"This is klarken ice!"

Jytte and Stellan forgot their aches and pains and began

dancing through the magic of the night, of the ice, of the nearness they felt to those great hunters and the possibility of finding their father.

Third sat down and crossed his legs, propping his chin on his forepaw as he regarded them. "I don't understand. What is this klarken ice and why is it so important?"

"We're going to find our father," Jytte explained. "And we were told we would be getting close to the hunting grounds when we began to see the klarken ice. *This* is klarken ice. You still want to come with us, don't you?"

"Of course. I certainly don't want to go back to Taaka. Nobody has cared for me at all until you two came along. I feel The Belong."

"The Belong? What's that?" Jytte asked.

"I think it's like love. But not quite the same." Third looked back over his shoulder. "I think I am caught between The Belong and danger. But if I, if we, have The Belong, I think we can face the danger."

The Belong. The words lingered in Stellan's and Jytte's minds. Was it a place? Or just a feeling?

CHAPTER 24

Blown Away

The klarken ice did not diminish but went on and on. Yet there was still no trace of the great hunters.

The sealing was good. With the strong winds, the snow was often blown off the ice in great swaths, and the cubs could see the seals swimming beneath the klarken. But even full bellies couldn't mask the concern that they were drifting farther from their father. Stellan had begun to wonder why there were no roarings in this region. If this was a place where the hunters gathered, why would they not celebrate with roarings?

On this particular day, the skies had darkened. There was a shift in the wind that seemed to resonate with a shift Stellan was feeling in himself as he gazed down at the red band timepiece.

"Seems like your plan is working out well, isn't it, Jytte?" Stellan asked with a slight sneer in his voice.

"Why say such a thing?"

"It's only a question, Jytte."

"He's just wondering," Third added. "I was wondering too. I asked Stellan the same thing the other night."

"Wondering what?" Jytte snapped. "And how dare you go behind my back, Stellan."

"You were sleeping! You want me to wake you up every time I speak to Third?"

"I don't like it when bears speak behind my back."

"It wasn't behind your back. You were asleep!"

"I wasn't asleep this morning when you said that we should head a bit more west. But that is not what Uluk Uluk said. We need to keep east of Nevermoves. East!" She raised her voice.

Stellan felt anger swelling in him. "WEST!" he shouted back. "Just try it — west. We're clearly not heading toward the hunting grounds. There's no sign of them!"

"I'm not risking that. EAST!"

Third clapped his paws over his ears. He couldn't stand it. He'd never seen the cubs fight before. Their faces became twisted and ugly. Their shouts scalded the air. He might have been back in the den with Taaka screaming at him. She often screamed at his brothers as well, even First, her favorite. She would slap them about, threatening to break their heads, tear out their claws. The horrible racket of that den, the sting of her swats all came back to him.

"STOP!" Third cried out. It was the anguish of his cry that stopped them. They looked at the cub. His paws were clamped over his ears. His eyes pinched shut for a moment, then he opened them slowly and looked from one cub to the other. "We have to stick together. We are all each other has."

"But you know nothing, Third. I know ice." Jytte's words were directed at Third, but she glared at her brother. She couldn't put up with this any longer. How dare they question her? How dare they try to keep her from finding her father? "EAST!" she shouted one more time, then bolted off, unable to stand it any longer.

"Jytte! Jytte!" Stellan called after her.

Suddenly, there was a deafening roar. The sky stirred with an odd color. Clouds streamed across the sky and a wind crashed down upon them. The blyndspryee! Stellan felt a thud against his chest. A blast of air had smacked Third against him. He clutched the little cub and opened his mouth to howl again for Jytte, but the howl was stuffed down his throat by the gusting wind. He began coughing. He dared not open his eyes, for the air had turned prickly with grit. He was accustomed to blinding snowstorms, but this was different. Where was Jytte? She was lighter than he was. Would she be blown to the Schrynn Gar, where she'd starve, scared and alone? He grasped Third harder, but his arms felt empty.

After what felt like ages, the roar of the blyndspryee began to diminish, until finally it was but a hoarse whisper leaving the gritty gray residue it had brought from across the Schrynn Gar. But for Stellan, the world was hollow. He stood up, shouting, bellowing his sister's name. If only she had not stomped off at just that moment. And to make matters worse, he had been left with the red band timepiece.

The world seemed directionless to Stellan. It was simply a void without his sister. Once, they had called everything that was different Not Mum. Well, this world was now Not Jytte. Not Jytte! This was impossible. They had always been together — always. There was never a night they had spent apart.

"We must find her," Third said. The little cub was pulling at his own ears, his eyes sliding back with terror. *I caused this . . . This is my fault*, Third thought.

"But where? Where do we start?" Stellan looked down at Third, whose white pelt was now dusky with the grit and dust.

Third said nothing but just began to walk. In a daze, Stellan followed the tiny cub. There was no hope of finding any tracks. The blyndspryee had erased every imprint and leveled any ice formations.

Jytte pulled herself out from beneath a low ice ledge where she'd eventually taken shelter once the wind grew too fierce.

The snow was gritty under her paws. Her fur was gritty and had turned gray. "Stellan! Stellan! Where . . . where are you?" But there was nothing but a resounding emptiness, only the sound of her own voice smacking against the klarken ice.

Fine, she thought. She'd be perfectly fine without her brother. How dare he doubt her? She would find her father on her own. He would recognize her instantly, of course. He would gather her into his arms. She would tell him about being an ice gazer. She might mention that Stellan was a riddler. She *might*. He'd ask where her brother and her mum were. And then because she was an ice gazer, she would lead him back to where Stellan and Third were. She'd have to explain about Third, but she was sure her father would understand. And then all of them would go to find Mum! But now she was tired and her shoulder was hurting her terribly. She had to take a little rest.

When she woke up hours later, a curious feeling came over her as she looked up at the sky. The stars were just where they should be. The Svree star pointing at Nevermoves, and the twin stars skipping between them, almost side by side. *But we're not side by side*, she thought. The words were like a stab in her heart.

She closed her eyes and tried not to cry. She regretted everything she had said to Stellan and Third. She hated herself. Hated that she was so impulsive, hated the recklessness that had brought her to this desolate place in this unknown world. She even hated her stupid dream of meeting her father.

Meeting him alone without her brother! How could she have ever dared to think of such a thing? She reached for the red band timepiece.

"Crow splat!" she muttered. Stellan had it. "Stellan!" she cried. She realized that the wind that had blown them apart had not been just any wind. It was the blyndspryee. She touched her head. There was a huge lump rising near her ear, and something sticky. She lowered her paw and saw a streak of blood. *I must have hit my head.* She recalled Uluk Uluk's words about these freakish winds, the blyndspryee. *You must grasp each other, clutch each other, for if you get separated, you might never find each other again.*

"Oh no!" Jytte crumpled to the ground. She touched the lump on her head, then spied nearby a rock with a blood smear on it. Her blood! Wherever they had been before the blyndspryee, there hadn't been any rocks. She must be some distance away from Stellan and Third. She could see the tops of two mountains. But were they mountains? They had the most bizarre shapes. Cones? Yes, the tops were like cones, and smoke was rising from them. Her mum had told her about such mountains. They were called volcanoes.

She pressed her paws to her eyes. How could this be happening? She had lost everything: her brother, the red band timepiece, her wits. How would she ever find her way out of this place? Would it be possible to retrace her steps back to Stellan and Third? But there were no steps. The blyndspryee had erased every paw print. At least it hadn't erased the stars. The stars still hung in the night sky. She could still find Nevermoves with or without the red band timepiece. And Stellan would still head north. He might not trust Uluk Uluk, but he would know that his sister would be heading north, for that star was all that bound them together now.

The wind began to blow a light, fresh breeze from a different direction. The red band in the sky became clearer. She could see a moon rising. She tried to picture the timepiece and where the hands had pointed the last time. *If I can see through snowdrifts and understand how crystals interlock, I should also be able to remember the parts of that timepiece, the hands and their positions the last time I saw them. I should be able to. I do have a brain. Let's see if it still works!*

CHAPTER 25

The Country of the Skulls

Through the rest of the night, Stellan and Third looked for Jytte. When they came across vast expanses of klarken ice uninterrupted by ridges of jumble ice, Stellan would hoist Third to his shoulders. The cub became adept at standing straight up while perched on his shoulders and peering into the distance — the emptiness, as Stellan thought of it, for there was no measure of distance that mattered in a world without his sister. But there was not a speck, not a bump on the horizon that could be Jytte. However, he refused to give up, and headed east. There must be a way to find her. The best plan was for him to head toward Oddsvall. That was the direction that Uluk Uluk had pointed them in. Surely Jytte would want to go there. She trusted Uluk Uluk. And so Stellan and Third continued on.

Stellan lost count of the days that had passed since the devouring wind, the blyndspryee, had swept away his sister. The sun never set, and the two cubs stopped as little as possible. Light flowed continuously across the land, and at *twiliqglow*, which lasted for long hours, the white pelts of the cubs turned golden in the setting sun. Stellan and Third swam down a gilded chukysh and climbed out onto a snowy bank. Checking the red band timepiece, Stellan lined up the hands with the glow on the horizon, then set the other hand exactly opposite to that one to set their course for tomorrow. But now there was no darkness to separate the tonights from the tomorrows. It was always today in the cubs' minds — an endless today with a sun that shone at midnight.

On the eve of the next day, Stellan and Third climbed out of the channel waters onto the gravelly banks of the eastern island as mist swirled around them. The mist quickly became so dense that they could hardly see to walk.

"Oddsvall?" Stellan murmured. "This is Oddsvall, I'm sure. The place that Uluk Uluk told us about."

Third gave a little shiver, a shiver of unease. He felt a disquiet seep through him but did not want to say anything yet.

"Look, the Schrynn Gar clouds!" Stellan exclaimed. "There's one that looks sort of like Jytte. You know how Jytte cocks her head sometimes." Stellan felt a lump swell in his throat. "Oh, Third, I can't stand it. I miss her so much. Maybe she's figured out how to come this way even without the red band."

"No!" Third barked.

"What are you talking about?"

Third had not meant to betray his doubts so quickly. He looked down at the ground and scuffed his foot in the snow, unable to meet Stellan's eyes. "I hope she is not coming this way." He tucked his chin into his shoulder as if he wanted the fur to muffle his words. "We . . . we need to turn around soon, as soon as we can. I think something is stalking us. I felt it as soon as we climbed up on this bank."

"A bear?"

Third's voice trembled with fear. "No. Like no other creature we have ever met. Not a toothwalker. Not a wolf. Something cunning. I can almost smell his cunning."

Stellan scowled at Third. "We can't turn around. I have a feeling Jytte is near. She might already be here." He continued walking, faster than before. He needed to find his sister.

"It's too dangerous," Third pleaded, running alongside Stellan.

Stellan skidded to a stop and planted himself directly in front of Third. "I won't turn around. I know you've never had a sister or brother who was kind to you. I know that Jytte and I fought sometimes. But the fights were nothing compared to our love. I simply can't turn around. I can't give up on my sister. And I know that she would never give up on finding me." He took a deep breath. "Third, if you want to turn back, you can. But I need to keep going."

"No, no, you don't understand at all." Third's eyes were wide with fear. "If we continue, I'm afraid neither of us will survive." His head drooped. "But I won't leave you. I am your brother. We go together."

The sight of the dejected cub made Stellan soften. "Oh, Third, I'm sorry. I didn't mean to insult you."

"Let's go on. We'll find her. Heart grit, remember? You're the one who told me of heart grit." But Third felt a curious commotion in his own heart that was more like a flutter than any grit. They had not walked far when Third stopped and, rising as tall as he could on his hind claws, pointed ahead.

"What is it?" Stellan called.

"I . . . I think it's a whale."

"But I don't smell any blubber," Stellan said, poking his nose into the air.

"There's no blubber to smell . . . just . . . just . . . bone," Third stammered. *This is a place of death!* But he knew there would be no discouraging Stellan.

Third scampered ahead and seemed to melt into the oblivion of the fog.

Through the veils of thickening mist, Stellan made his way and found the cub standing on tippy claws against a whale skull and peering into the void of the eye socket. The fog suddenly cleared, and the two cubs found themselves standing in a half circle of immense whale skulls.

"Something happened here . . . ," Third said, looking about.

"I'll say." Stellan was standing by a pile of immense sun-bleached bones on the outside of the half circle. He picked up a long stick with a sharp point. "What do you call this?"

"Dangerous!" Third replied. He slid his dark eyes around as if expecting something to snatch him by the throat.

Stellan looked at the point. Although rusted, it was still sharp. "They killed whales here."

"They?" Third asked.

"The Others." Stellan swung his head toward a post with writing, and began to sound out the letters. "Odds — Oddsvall!" Stellan exclaimed. "We've arrived!" He looked from side to side, desperate for a sign of Jytte. *She has to be here.* The words rang in Stellan's head like a mournful tolling. *She has to be.*

CHAPTER 26

Two Trails Meet

Jytte tried not to think about Stellan and Third, because when she thought about them, she imagined them lost forever or in some sort of terrible danger, and the pain was too much to bear.

For six nights she traveled alone. At least she knew that she had traveled the right course. She no longer needed the red band timepiece. It seemed that it had embedded itself in her head. She had also become more adept at navigating by the stars. She looked for her father's star in the knee of the Great Bear and then the one in the forward paw that pointed to Nevermoves. She found the twin stars as well. Perhaps that was a sign that she and Stellan were not that far apart even if they were not together. But on these pale nights the stars were often hard to see and did not last long.

She wished she hadn't always taken her big brother for granted. They were so different, but that was what she missed most of all. She was foolish for railing at him for his worrying, his caution. There was, it seemed to Jytte, a space in this world that could not be filled.

She was now climbing up a steep and very icy path. It had begun to snow lightly. The two volcanoes were shrouded with mist and there was an icy great peak of some sort in between, but it was difficult to see it in the ever-increasing fog. As she climbed, she began to pick up an odd odor, an odor that reminded her of Moon Eyes. She bent down and scraped up some snow. She gasped. *Issen blauen.* The same ice that filled his empty eye sockets. Issen blauen was a singular ice. *It only occured . . .* Jytte's mind seemed to stumble, but she forced herself to think. It only occurred at the Ice Cap. *A bad place. Bad bears who tore the eyes out of good bears . . . bears like Moon Eyes!* A terrible thought sent her reeling. *Stellan was right!* Uluk Uluk had betrayed them. She felt a hot anger boil up in her.

Great Ursus! I'm in the Ublunkyn! Uluk Uluk has sabotaged us. He sent us in the wrong direction. Aghast, Jytte looked about. There were only volcanoes and mountains. She was as far away as one could be from the sea and the sealing grounds. She looked ahead, where occasionally the fog would thin, and there would be blinding flashes of reflected light off the peak.

It was hard to imagine what could burn so brightly. She could never quite see it before another stampede of clouds would hurl in and obscure the peak. But she was too frightened and angry to think much of it. She had to get away from this terrible place. She had to find Stellan and Third before it was too late.

High in the Ice Clock were four towers where Issengards stood watch.

"Hvrak, come over here. The fog's cleared. Take a look." A bear with a slight limp went to the issen blauen scope, where a she-bear had her eye pressed.

Despite his stiff hip, Hvark's eyes were as sharp as youngsters'. "Interesting."

"Can you make it out?" the she-bear asked.

"Three cubs, two on the east trail, one on the west trail."

"How did they find us?"

"I don't think they found us," Hvrak replied. "But we'll find them. Send out two teams of Roguers."

The fog grew thinner as Stellan and Third wound their way up the path. They were approaching the summit where an immense structure glared in the dawn light. They had noticed icy spines — narrow bridges — reaching across the deep abyss that separated the trail from the two volcanoes. The spines shimmered and appeared as delicate as the bones of a small fragile bird. The Schrynn Gar clouds still blew overhead.

"What is that?" Stellan whispered. It looked as if all the intricate pieces of clockwork in Uluk Uluk's laboratory had reassembled themselves here on this mountaintop. But these pieces were *huge*. There was a clock face as wide as a broad river, with four enormous dials on it. Like a wisp torn loose from a windblown cloud, a dim cry threaded through Stellan's mind. *Don't go! Don't go!* It was the echo of his own voice crying for his mother not to leave. A scent that he had known forever swirled through his head. There was only one word for these fleeting impressions — *Mum!* Could she be near? Why else would he think of her right now? *Mum*, he thought desperately. *Help us, please!*

At the very same moment, Jytte was staring ahead, stunned. She shook her head fiercely as if to clear it. *I must be dreaming*, she thought. But then out of the corner of her eye she caught a fragment of something, just the shadow of a movement, something dimly familiar. Jytte opened her eyes wide. It was her brother! And Third!

"Stellan!" she cried. She raced down to where the two trails met at a turnoff.

"Jytte!" Stellan roared as an indescribable joy flooded through him. He and Third ran toward Jytte and embraced.

And at just that moment, the shadows of four Roguers slipped over the freshly fallen snow.

CHAPTER 27

On the Spine

As the three cubs ran, Jytte glanced back over her shoulder at the advancing Roguer bears, then ahead at the ice spines that arced high into the air, stretching across a seemingly bottomless abyss. It became immediately clear that the only way to escape the Roguers was to run along one of the ice spines that spanned the deep ravine. These slender bows of ice would never sustain the weight of a full-grown bear, but the lighter cubs might have a chance. A chance they must take. Because rushing toward them were the infamous Roguers that Moon Eyes had told them about.

Ahead were the silver spines of ice. Below, the earth fell away into a vast depth and certain death. Stellan gasped. "How? How will we ever get across?" In order to get onto one of the spines, they'd have to jump.

"Follow me!" Third shouted, and then made a spectacular leap through the air. He landed on the ice spine that connected the mountain they were on with the volcano.

Jytte held her breath. To her relief, she saw that the spindle of ice was holding Third's weight.

"Follow him?" Stellan peered into the ravine and felt a dizzying swirl. It was as if the world fell away completely. His legs felt weak, like every single bone in his body was melting. He clamped his eyes shut. He simply could not look down. "Won't it break?"

"No, it won't. It can hold us and hopefully not them," Jytte said, glancing back at the four Roguer bears. But despite her words, her voice trembled. Then she shrieked as she saw two bears begin to swirl a net in the air.

"Jump! Jump!" Third cried out as the filigree of the net printed against the morning sky.

The two cubs locked eyes for a brief moment, then ran toward the sliver of ice.

Stellan felt the muscles in his hind legs gather, the ones in his shoulders stretch. He did not think — he just leaped. There was a dizzying moment of weightlessness as he launched himself into thin air.

Then he heard a creak. A creak and not a crack. Then a second creak. Did that mean they both had landed? *It must*, Stellan thought, and looked back and saw his sister straddling the ice spine.

Third looked over his shoulder at the cubs. "Slide!" he commanded. "Slide across on your bellies. Don't look down."

Stellan willed himself not to look, as the drop into the abyss was enormous. He could hear the Roguers talking, and their voices propelled him onward. *Don't look down. Don't look back!*

"The next spine over could hold you, Jart. You're the lightest," one of the Roguers said.

"That spine is not that thin, Jart. You'll do fine. Take the net to use when you get close to them."

"Keep going!" Third said. "Keep going. Don't listen to them, just concentrate."

"Spread your weight if you can, Stellan," Jytte said. "Straddle the spine." She had closed her eyes tightly, and in her mind's eye, she could see precisely how this ice was structured, exactly how the crystals locked together.

Stellan grew alarmed as the ice spine seemed to grow narrower as he inched his way across the the great abyss. He was not at the halfway point yet, but the spine started to arc upward at a steep angle.

"We must go slower. The ice is more fragile. The crystals . . ." Jytte's voice trailed off. She felt her heart beat faster as her breath grew shallow. She knew that this slender sliver of ice could snap any second. But instead of thinking about that, she had to focus on what she knew about ice. She must let the ice tell her its story. "We can't all reach the top at once. I can hear cracklings in the spine. I can smell it melting as the sun rises and the ice wears thin. Third, you go over the summit first. Then Stellan, but wait until Third is almost across. Then I'll come. Understand?"

"Yes," the other two cubs replied. Behind them, they could hear slaps of the nets being flung out vainly by the Roguers. Thankfully, their aim was not good. But occasionally the edge of the net would hit their ice spine and the cubs would feel a shudder.

Behind them, the Roguers were arguing. They were still trying to convince the bear Jart to climb out onto one of the other spines.

"Jart, that spine, the next one over, is stronger, I can tell," one was saying. "If you go out on that with a net, you'll bag one of them."

"So I get to die trying to get these cursed cubs? Just to get a few more Tick Tocks?"

Third shuddered at the sound of the words *Tick Tock*. He saw the blood that had seeped into his mother's dreams. He was almost at the top of the spine, but he was quivering so hard he could barely grip with his knees. The ice had grown slick as the sun rose. He felt his grip weakening. He was sliding back. If he slid into Stellan, it would be too much weight at a critical point.

"Don't slide back, Third! Hold on tighter!" Jytte barked.

Third gripped the slender spine with all his might and climbed upward. Only when he reached the top could he loosen his aching grip and let himself slide down the other side.

He was doing it. He was not sure how. But his clasp was holding. He began to slide, and within seconds bumped onto land. *I'm across!* A few moments later, Stellan arrived. As he scrambled to his feet, both cubs turned to look for Jytte.

To their dismay, they saw she was not yet at the top of the arc. The Roguer bears were cheering on Jart, who was on the next spine over.

"That's it, Jart! Good fellow. I knew you could do it." The bear Jart was as tall as he was slender. Balancing on the ice spine next to Jytte's, he stood up to his full height and began to swing the net above his head. Jytte froze as she saw the tracery of dark mesh drift languidly against the azure sky. It was plummeting toward her like a circle of death. She had only a split second to escape it. Without thinking, she slung herself under the ice spine and hung on by her claws, upside down. The net hit the spine. She felt the mesh drag across the tops of her claws, but it did not snag them.

"Try it again. Try it again!" the other Roguers roared.

"You can make it, Jytte, you can!" Third called to her.

"Not far, Jytte. Stay upside down," Stellan urged.

Jart let out a frustrated growl. "I'll get her. I'll get her next time."

Fury rose in Stellan, boiling anger like he had never known. There was a good-size rock where he stood on the slope of the volcano. He reached down and picked it up. He narrowed his eyes and calculated the distance. He didn't have much time.

Jart was gathering in the net to cast it again. Just as Jart lifted his arm into the air, Stellan threw the rock. There was a soft thud as the rock hit the top of Jart's head. The net fell from his paw into the abyss. Jart began to wobble. A strange quavery roar came from deep in his lungs: "Ah . . . a . . . aaah . . ." Stellan watched with a mix of satisfaction and horror as the Roguer fell off the spine and began plummeting through the air. So deep was the abyss that the sound when the bear hit the ground was hardly more than a muffled thunk. In this distance, he heard the other Roguers let out muffled screams and curses.

Jytte slid down the ice spine onto the slope of the volcano. Safe at last. Stellan cried out with happiness and swept her into his arms. Third clung to her knees, his face wet with tears. They stood back to look at one another and stared gasping in disbelief. The agony of separation was over. They pawed one another's fur as if to confirm that this was real, that these were not apparitions. That they were together again.

"Uluk Uluk betrayed us," Jytte said, her voice ragged. "Uluk Uluk drove us toward the Roguers. Look at this place — volcanoes. It's far from the sea. Why would our father be hunting here?" She paused and inhaled deeply, trying to catch her breath. "And that!" Jytte said, pointing to the Ice Clock, which was clearly visible now. "That is an evil place. I'm sure of it."

They looked up at the monster clock that radiated a brutal glittering light, a fiendish wrath, as if it were waiting to devour the world.

CHAPTER 28

The Gilly Forest

The cubs breathed a sigh of relief when they saw the first signs of trees. They were rather small, wispy things, but they meant the cubs were approaching the tree line and heading south.

But for Third, the relief did not last long. As soon as they began winding their way through a thin forest with stunted trees, he felt a sickening apprehension. He said nothing at first, though Stellan sensed Third's anxiety. Silence fell upon all of them as a vaporous mist began to swirl through the dwarf trees.

"Are these really trees?" Stellan asked. "Remember that tree Mum showed us? It was huge. These look more like weeds."

"And these don't have bark. Their trunks and branches look like bones," Jytte replied. She reached out and touched the silvery-gray trunk of the closest tree. "Oh, Ursus, like gillys! It's a gillygaskin forest."

Third looked around. "Hush!" he whispered.

Stellan and Jytte stopped abruptly. The little cub sensed things the other two never could, not even with their gifts of being an ice gazer and a riddler.

"What's wrong?" Stellan asked.

"Something is following us," Third replied.

"A Roguer?" Jytte asked, and tried to block the image of that net printed against the sky.

"No . . . It's a different sound." Stellan and Jytte both cocked their heads. "It moves much differently from any bear."

"A wolf?" Jytte asked nervously.

"No. Bigger but quiet, sly."

Jytte and Stellan exchanged glances. They were not relieved.

The three cubs continued haltingly, pausing every time Third stopped to look around.

"I hear it and then I don't. It moves when we're moving and stays still when we are still. It's as if a shadow is following us."

A shadow? Jytte thought. *This isn't good. Are we being stalked?* Perhaps it was Uluk Uluk himself. Jytte felt a flash of fear and turned to Stellan. She was about to speak the terrible bear's name, but she dared not. To name him was to make him come to life here in this gillygaskin forest.

They continued on for a good stretch before Third paused again. "I think it's stopped following us," he said tentatively.

"Look, a sign," Jytte whispered. It was propped against a large pile of brush. "Syvert Hansen's Dry Goods, since 1862."

Third scampered closer. "Syvert. Is that close to your father's name?"

"You mean Svern. Yes, he — "

"Hello there," a deep but calm voice interrupted. It was unlike any voice they had ever heard. Not bear. Not seal. Not wolf. The three cubs stopped in their tracks.

A creature stepped forward from behind the brush pile. He was lithe and moved with an ineffably supple grace. His fur sheathed him in a frosty radiance of silver and mystery.

"I am Skagen. You have never seen my like?"

"Never!" Stellan finally managed.

The cubs could have never even imagined such an animal. He was solidly build but seemed to flow like water over the ground. His eyes were a strange, luminous green with flecks of gold. "I am a snow leopard."

The cubs were mesmerized as they watched the creature draw closer. He fixed the three cubs in the blue-green light of his tilting eyes.

"Follow me," Skagen said, and then with his mouth he pulled away a rusted sheet of metal, then kicked aside some boards.

But the cubs stood rooted to the ground. They had been deceived once. Why should they trust this snow leopard? They looked at one another desperately. Each had the same thought. Behind them were the Roguers. Ahead of them was this unimaginable creature. He was certainly as frightening as any Roguer. Muscles rippled beneath his sleek pelt. His fangs were long and sharp as any bear's.

"Come. You'll be Roguer bait out here. They'll never find you if you follow me."

"It's a trick," Jytte cautioned the other cubs hoarsely.

"A trick? If I wanted to kill you, I could do it right here. Now come along. Follow me. Concealment is crucial. Kindly pass ahead and stop at the first *kapunquat*."

Jytte looked at Stellan as if to say, *Should we?* Stellan tipped his head and nodded almost imperceptibly, but she saw assurance in his eyes.

They followed Skagen. The cave was combed with ice spears that glittered and reflected different colors as light seeped in from some invisible source. The path twisted and sometimes dipped steeply, then would begin to rise again. At times there were spaces that opened up off the narrow path into coves that pooled with water. But there were also overhangs that nearly obscured the cave's ceiling. It was a curious place indeed, with crystal formations that often towered over them, and despite the dimness it seemed to glow as if it had captured its own sun. It wasn't quite night or full day. They felt as if they had entered a different world. The cubs followed, mesmerized by the rhythmic sway of the snow leopard's tail and the sleek elegance of his motions.

Third said quietly, "I dreamed of this place a few days before we climbed out at Oddsvall. I didn't know what it was then. And now . . . now I do."

"What is it?" Stellan asked.

"The Cave of Lost Time," Third whispered.

"Not exactly," the snow leopard said, twisting his head around to look at them.

"What, then?" Third asked.

"You're a bold cub for one so small." Skagen stopped and turned about.

Third wrinkled his brow. He knew he was much smaller than Jytte and Stellan, but it seemed unnecessary to comment on it.

"Sorry," the snow leopard replied. "Size has nothing to do with it." Third nodded. "But to answer your question, time cannot be lost. It can be unaccounted for, but not really lost. And of all places to call lost or to associate with lost time, this is the last one. For indeed time has been *found* here. This, young'uns, is the Cave of Svree."

"Svree?" Jytte repeated, as the word echoed as if from afar. That a creature who was not a bear should speak it seemed strange and yet wonderful.

"Who is Svree?" Third asked.

Svree. Jytte and Stellan looked at each other as the meaning of that name burned brightly in their minds. They remembered what their mum had told them, that the pointer star in the paw of the constellation shared the same name as their great-great-grandfather Svree.

"He was a bear of Nunquivik like yourselves," Skagen said. "And he wanted to stop the murder of innocents."

Stellan shivered as he saw what was in Skagen's mind — cubs. Cubs that were bleeding and mangled and missing paws and legs. Cubs that were dying on a wheel spiked with teeth.

"They call them Tick Tocks," Skagen continued quietly.

"I saw them!" Third squealed in horror. "I saw them in Taaka's dreams. Tick Tocks. I was to be a Tick Tock."

"Aaah!" The sound rumbled up from deep within the snow leopard. "So you have the hidden eye, cub!" He paused. "Or perhaps the dream eye, and some might call it the third eye."

Jytte glared at Skagen. "Don't try to flatter us. That's what Uluk Uluk did. He told us we were special. We're not going to fall for that again."

The snow leopard stared at her, a sudden flash of anger illuminating his green eyes. "You know Uluk Uluk?"

Stellan nodded, recoiling slightly at Skagen's expression. "He told us he would help us find our father. But instead, he sent us far off course. That's how the Roguers almost captured us."

Skagen sighed, his eyes softening. "You are right about Uluk Uluk. You were merely his tool. Nothing more. He cared not a whit about you finding your mum or your father. He is not evil, but he has no heart left. It was shattered many years ago."

CHAPTER 29

Divine and Evil — Strange Denmates

The passageways became more tangled as they followed Skagen. The strange frost spears, kapunquats, descended from the ceiling and erupted from the floor.

"How do you know Uluk Uluk?" Jytte asked, her mind whirling with questions.

"Let's wait until we're all the way inside," Skagen said. "Voices carry in this cave, and we don't know who might be lingering outside." He pointed toward a narrow passageway. Those are *heligs*, which means 'death air.' Very dangerous. Avoid them. The strange thing is that close to the heligs are tunnels with clear air. If you can get to a clear air passage quickly, you can recover."

The three cubs followed silently. The cave contained a wondrous and mystical world. The crystal formations cast a radiance of colors — some shimmered quietly, some glowed, and some burst with vigor. It felt as if the dancing lights of the ahalikki had flowed from the sky deep into the earth.

They descended a series of polished white steps that led to an immense space. At one end they saw an ice bridge suspended over a pool. There was a familiar soft jingling sound. Dripping from the ceiling were clusters of very slender kapunquats. Their reflections stippled the water of the pool. But also reflected in the mirror of water were shapes they had seen before, the source of the jingling.

"Gears," Stellan whispered. "This is like Uluk Uluk's cell six, but much bigger."

"Indeed." Skagen stepped onto the ice bridge and looked down on them from above. "The escapement wheel — the beating heart of every clock. The one that too many cubs have died on. Too many Tick Tocks."

Third began to tremble and pressed against Stellan's leg.

The clock pieces quivered in the windless space, twinkling between the threads of the glowing worms. The snow leopard descended from the ice bridge, his shadow undulating across the spears he called kapunquats.

"Tell me how you encountered Uluk Uluk, and I'll tell you all I know as well." Jytte and Stellan exchanged a nervous glance. Something told them they could trust this creature, but they'd been betrayed so many times before. Stellan cleared his throat and told Skagen about their mum, how'd she left them with Taaka to go to the Den of Forever Frost. Then Jytte cut in and explained what happened with Uluk Uluk, how his directions had led them to the terrifying place where the Roguers lurked.

Skagen was silent for a long time before he spoke. "I think Uluk Uluk believed that you, Jytte and Stellan, have a gift. He sent you in the wrong direction for a good cause. He wanted you to break the clock and save the Tick Tocks from the tyranny of the Timekeepers. But it's not worth risking your lives for such a difficult, dangerous mission. At least, I don't think so. There is a better way."

"But why has this happened? Why are they doing this to those poor cubs?" Stellan asked.

"A long time ago, the good bear Svree, that some called the Thief of Time, began his life's work right here in this cave. Svree's work was the creation of the Ice Clock. A clock that would help us calculate the next Great Melting, the greatest disaster of the Long Ago. Little would he dream that a worse disaster was coming, when bears would begin to sacrifice their own."

"Svree! That's our ancestor!" Jytte cut in.

Skagen gave her a strange look. "Indeed? What is your mother's name, cub?"

"Our mother is Svenna and our father is Svern."

"Svern . . . ," Skagen whispered.

"It is!" Jytte said forcefully.

"Is . . . is something wrong?" Stellan asked.

"No . . . ," Skagen said hoarsely. "Nothing . . . I just never . . . never . . ."

"Never what?" asked Jytte.

The snow leopard shook his head as if to rid himself of whatever thoughts were troubling him. "As I was saying, years later, the bears of the Ice Cap began to ask things of the clock that were beyond its power. They could not accept that such a grand mechanical creation couldn't answer all their questions, solve all their problems, and dispel all of their fears. The Timekeepers became superstitious and began to worry that they had wronged the clock in some way. So they started to worship the clock like a god. A false god. They thought this false god demanded sacrifice and tribute. And then and only then would it disclose the secrets it had kept from them. It is curious, but some creatures need their devils as much as their gods. Know this, cub." The green light in his eyes glowed fiercely. "The divine and the evil often den together. Yes, strange denmates, but nonetheless they have a peculiar attraction for each other."

"You see, cubs" — he looked at Stellan and Jytte as he spoke — "it is my belief that the Roguers took your mum." Jytte let out a gasp, but Stellan merely stared straight ahead. He realized that ever since he saw those Roguers at the ice spine, that notion had been buried deep in his mind. "She went in your place. That happens sometimes, especially if the mother is smart, as I'm sure your mother is."

"Did they make her a Tick Tock?" The words seemed to almost strangle Jytte as she spoke. Terror filled her eyes. Stellan reached out and clutched her paw.

"Oh no, only cubs. They most likely put her to work as a numerator."

"Would that be safe?" Stellan asked.

"No one is ever safe at the Ice Cap," Skagen said grimly.

Stellan gripped Jytte's paw tighter.

"How can we save her? Free her?" Stellan asked.

"You can't free her until you save your own kind." Skagen paused. "In order to save the bear world, you must break the clock. And to do this, you must find your father, Svern."

CHAPTER 30

Teach Us, Then, Skagen

The cubs stared at Skagen, dumbstruck. "Our father?" Jytte repeated hoarsely. "What does he have to do with the clock?"

"Everything!" Skagen replied. "You see, your father saw what was happening to the bear world. He attempted to end the tyranny of the clock, of the Timekeepers. He nearly succeeded in destroying the clock but was almost caught and had to flee to the Den of Forever Frost."

"But our mum said he went north to hunt. She would have never lied to us," Stellan said.

"I'm sure she didn't. He might have told her that was his reason for heading north."

"But it wasn't?" Jytte asked weakly.

"No; you see, your father was the leader of the rebellion. Although the Bear Council had long been disbanded, a group of brave bears took it upon themselves to stand up to the Timekeepers, to demand that they release the Tick Tocks and the other captive creatures. When the Timekeepers refused, your father decided he had to break the clock, to prove it was only a false god. He sneaked into the Ice Cap undercover and nearly succeeded, but he was betrayed. He had to flee. He barely escaped with his life."

"How do you know all this?" Jytte asked, narrowing her eyes.

"Because I too was part of the rebellion," Skagen said, raising his chin. "Although I am a snow leopard, I was proud to fight for such a noble cause."

"So you know our father? You know where to find him?" Jytte asked eagerly.

Skagen shook his head as the fierce light in his eyes dimmed slightly. "I knew him. I was honored to fight alongside him. But I haven't seen him since he fled somewhere near the Den of Forever Frost. No one has seen him."

"Is . . . is he okay? Is he hurt?" Stellan asked, afraid to look at his sister.

"I'm not sure. All I know is that, without him, the rebellion stands no chance. We need your father. And you, cubs, have to be the ones to find him."

"Us?" Jytte and Stellan exchanged startled looks.

"Yes. Only you, his cubs, can convince him to rejoin the fight."

"But you'll help us get there, right?" Stellan asked. He and Jytte had barely survived their journey from Nunquivik. How could they possibly go so much farther on their own?

He shook his head. "Only bears can enter the Den of Forever Frost. It would violate the long-standing treaty between the bears and the snow leopards, if I came with you. But I will give you a map to help you on your journey."

"Teach us, then, Skagen," Jytte said. "Teach us how to read the map so we can find the Den of Forever Frost and our father."

"Come this way."

They followed him to a long ice slab where maps had already been spread. "I had some visitors a few days ago. Bears who've been looking for your father. But I haven't heard a word from them. It's possible they were captured by the enemy."

Skagen unfurled another map, this one very ancient in appearance. He anchored it with a small rock at each corner. "This is Ga'Hoole." He pointed with a claw to a vast region that almost encircled a sea. "This land north of Ga'Hoole is the Northern Kingdoms. It used to be called the N'yrthghar in ancient times. The time of your ancestor Svree. You see how these kingdoms were separated from Ga'Hoole proper by straits — the ice narrows that run between the Sea of Hoolemere and that known as the Everwinter Sea. That is where the bear kingdoms of Ga'Hoole are."

The cubs hunched over the large work slab, listening eagerly as Skagen showed them how to find the Den of Forever Frost.

Inside the cave, it was impossible to tell day from night, but after a few hours, Stellan and Jytte started to yawn, and Third fell asleep with his face on one of the maps.

Skagen gently picked up Third by the scruff of his neck and carried him to a pile of furs, then gestured to another pile where Jytte and Stellan could sleep. This time, they did not argue about whether to trust Skagen. Gratefully, they curled up and drifted to sleep, feeling safe and warm for the first time since their mum had left.

Over the next several days, Skagen taught them how to plot out a true navigational course with a compass and a sextant. The red band timepiece was still helpful, but with the additional navigational skills that Skagen was teaching them, they would be prepared for their journey to the bear kingdoms of Ga'Hoole with much better accuracy.

After a long evening of studying maps, the cubs and Skagen gathered to have cocoa. The cubs loved the sweet drink and enjoyed preparing it.

"Do you want your usual, Skagen?" Third inquired.

"Yes, Third, but just a touch of the schnapps."

"Just a touch," Third replied. After he had poured it into the cocoa, he looked at the label. "You call it schnapps, but here on the label they call it *aquavit*."

"Call it what you will, it tastes disgusting," Jytte said,

making a face. "When I tried it, it burned my throat right down past my belly and into my claws."

"It's not for young'uns," Skagen said. "And I'm old." His muzzle had become quite gray in the past year, and he felt a crick in his hip. He wondered if Uluk Uluk was feeling the years as well.

"No you're not!" Jytte said forcefully. The snow leopard looked across at them. Their dark eyes were always shiny, so ready to learn. Teaching these cubs about the maps and navigation, living with them in the cave, had been one of the happiest periods in Skagen's life.

CHAPTER 31

Never to Rise

"You are ready," Skagen announced one evening as the cubs pored over unrolled scrolls of maps and charts in a small chamber that Skagen called the library. It was a cozy chamber, and they often sipped their cocoa from shallow rock cups lined with crystals that Skagen told them were geodes. They were always careful not to spill any on the maps.

"Are you sure?" Stellan asked, slurping a mouthful of cocoa from his geode, which was lined with lavender and yellow crystals.

"But you won't go with us?" Jytte asked. They had grown very fond of the snow leopard.

He shook his head. "No. This is your history; your stories are waiting for you in the Den of Forever Frost. You are the cubs of Svern and the great-great-grandcubs of both Svarr and Svree, the noblest and the most courageous of bears. If you can find the Den of Forever Frost, if any part of it still exists, this is your destiny. And then and only then will you be able to break the clock."

"I think we're ready," Jytte said quickly. "I remember what we are supposed to do. We watch the star in the tip of the Fighting Bear constellation." She leaned over a star chart she was studying. "Here it is." She pointed with her claw to the starry configuration that resembled a bear striding across the night sky.

"And what stars will you begin to see as you travel south in addition to the Fighting Bear?"

"The Great Claw constellation," Stellan replied quickly, pointing to another on his sister's chart.

"And what do the owls call that constellation?"

"The Golden Talons," Third replied. He held up his paw. "Owls have talons; we have claws. I can't wait to see an owl!"

"You'll see plenty when you head south to the Ga'Hoolian kingdoms."

"Indeed. See, you all have learned so much. You have the star maps as well as these maps in your head. You will all be great navigators. You should leave soon, but before you go, I plan to make a visit to Syvert's and bring you back some of Granny Solveig's Best Cocoa. I know how much you like it."

"Love it!" Jytte exclaimed.

"And it will give you energy for your journey."

So the following evening, Skagen left for Syvert Hansen's store. He had kept his old habits from the Schrynn Gar, where the snow leopards mostly hunted "on the *cresp*" — the edges of dawn and twiliqglow. Not that one had to be especially strategic when the prey was a twelve-ounce can of Granny Solveig's Best Cocoa, "The Best Money Can Buy," whatever money was. Nevertheless, he wanted to arrive at dawn. So he gave the sleeping cubs a lick with his big rough tongue and left.

By the break of first light, Skagen had wended his way through Oddsvall and was now approaching the northern outskirts. The funny little building of Syvert Hansen's Dry Goods store appeared. It seemed so sad, warped by the wind and leaning wearily against the landscape. The metal roof slid off to one side. The sign that once had been nailed above the entry had been torn off years before, and Skagen had dragged it back to the cave to camouflage the opening. He wandered through, pulling a bag he'd fashioned from the stomach of a seal.

Skagen examined all the shelves — half of them empty, as many of the tinned goods had fallen off over the years. But it always paid to look up, and not just down. The shelves weren't that high, so anything he wanted was in easy reach. He spotted a box of Onkel Rolvag's Oatmeal. He loved oatmeal, and the cubs had never tasted it. There were also several small tins of sardines. Jytte especially liked those. Tricky, however, to open. One had to use one's small teeth in the back to puncture the tin and then tear with the tiny flip claw to peel back the top.

Next, he went over to a bin that held odds and ends. He picked through an assortment of tins, bottles, and small boxes. He liked the bottles, for the glass could be useful. He picked up one. *Lydia Pinkham's Tonic for Female Complaints.* Too bad it was dark purple glass. It would never suffice for a watch lens. The numbers would not be visible through the glass. But he had found two tins of Granny Solveig's Best Cocoa. And three tins of Papa Van Stokel's Pork and Beans. Just as he was reaching for the third tin, he heard a noise. Then a shadow slid across the floor.

He spun around. Three immense figures blocked the breaking light in the east. Skagen felt the blood freeze in his veins. He could smell the bloody banners that were emblazoned on their chests. He knew that his own blood might be added to this display.

"Come out!" one roared.

Skagen snarled.

"We smell the cubs on you. The Grand Patek demands fresh cubs."

"Never!" Skagen roared back. He would fight. He felt his muscles coiling beneath his pelt. He would strike for their hearts.

The huge bears, many times larger than Skagen, tore off the frame of the entry. A wall collapsed. Stones began tumbling down on him. He had no choice. He leaped through the opening and was immediately tackled.

The largest bear put his paw on Skagen's neck. "The cubs! The cubs! Tell us where they are or prepare to die."

The bear's foot was crushing his windpipe, and Skagen's limbs began to jerk in wild spasms as he fought for breath. If he died, they would find their way to the cubs. If the cubs died . . . no, this could not happen.

He was losing consciousness, but he had to keep fighting. He had to. Feeling a surge of energy, Skagen twisted under the weight and managed to sink his fangs into the top of the bear's paw. He heard a yowl. The ground beneath him quaked and the snow turned red. Skagen managed to drag himself out from under the attacking bear. *I shall not die. I shall not die.* He heard the continuous roaring of the maddened bear, which reverberated all the way to the inlet and shattered the newly formed ice. Two other bears stood by, momentarily stunned that their leader had been wounded.

"Attack! Attack, you fools!" the wounded bear bellowed.

Skagen felt the ground quake again as the two bears stormed him. One lunged. There was a resounding smack followed by a crack. Skagen collapsed. This time he knew he would never rise again.

"Don't kill him," one bear said. "We need him to take us to the cubs."

"Don't worry. We'll find his tracks. This snow is fresh." The lead bear of the Roguers, a she-bear named Enka, replied confidently as she stepped harder on Skagen's spine.

Skagen felt no pain. Just a creeping numbness. Another bear knelt down. "Ready to talk?"

Skagen's breath was labored. He looked into the bear's eyes. "I have nothing to say to you," he whispered, and died.

CHAPTER 32

The Cubs Worry

Jytte tapped on the tin of Granny Solveig's cocoa. "I just don't understand," she said grumpily. "It never takes Skagen this long."

"You know that snow leopards like to travel at twiliqglow. He might have waited," Third said. He was poring over a map of the Northern Kingdoms of Ga'Hoole.

Stellan was by his side and pointed with a claw to a long, narrow inlet. "They call those *firths* in Ga'Hoole. Mum told us that."

"Why don't they call them channels or chukyshes the way we do here?" Third asked.

"They're different. Very deep, and there are always high cliffs around them. Once they might have been valleys."

"How can you two just keep talking about that map?" Jytte snapped. "It's late now and he's not back."

By midnight, the cubs were truly frightened. They had forgotten all about cocoa and the maps.

"Should we go out and hunt for him?" Jytte asked.

"Skagen told us very specifically that we should never go near Oddsvall, not since those Roguers nearly caught us. Too close to the ice spines," Stellan said.

"But this is an emergency. What if he's hurt?" Jytte whimpered.

"He is kind of old," Third said. "I know his hip was bothering him the other day. I saw him limping."

"Limping? Really?" Stellan was astonished. "I always think of him as moving so smoothly. It's as if he melts through air."

A tear began to roll down Jytte's face. Stellan was right. Skagen was the most graceful creature on earth.

Stellan suddenly sniffed. "What's that scent?"

"What scent?" Third said.

Great vapors of smoke were rolling into the cave. All three cubs thought of the heligs, the passages with their death air, that Skagen had warned them about.

"Clear air . . . we must . . . get to the clear tunnel . . . near here, I think," Jytte gasped. She was coughing. She tried to hold her breath but couldn't, yet every time she breathed, it seared her throat. She staggered, then fell to her knees. "Stellan!

Stellan!" she gasped again, and reached out for her brother. But there was nothing.

Outside the cave, the Roguers who had murdered Skagen, Jost and Enka, had set coals from the twin volcanoes Prya and Pupya in small holes in the ground. Fanning them, they sent drafts of the smoke into the cave.

"The wind is in our favor," Enka said. "It'll help us. The Ice Clock is pleased, and so the wind comes!"

"Aye." Jost nodded. "The Ice Clock is pleased."

They began to chant as the smoke swirled into the cave.

"The cubs will rush out soon," Enka continued. "Casters stand alert." She nodded to two bears with nets. "Hakon, ready your scimitar claws. The cubs must serve the clock or die."

"The cubs must serve the clock or die," repeated the other bears like a death chorus.

Enka craned her head on her long neck forward, turning to see into the mouth of the cave. She was growing impatient. "Time check?" she demanded.

"Eighteen minutes, twenty-four seconds, and five milliseconds."

The cubs should have come out by now. But there was no sign of them.

"Here! Here!" Third said in a rasping voice. "This is the clear tunnel." Jytte dragged herself forward, clamping her mouth shut so as not to breathe in the smoke. She heard Stellan beside her, coughing and choking. But finally there was a blast of crisp, cold air. They all inhaled huge drafts of the fresh air as they tumbled into the narrow space, gasping with relief. Their heads began to clear. Their sluggish bodies quickened. But outside the helig, they could see that the cave was still roiling with smoke.

They were trapped.

CHAPTER 33

A Spirit Guide?

"Will we be stuck here forever?" Jytte asked, her voice raw from the smoke.

"We can't go out the usual way. There will still be smoke," Stellan replied hoarsely.

"And they will still be there," Third added.

"Who?" Jytte said.

"Roguers from the Ice Cap," Stellan said faintly. "They're waiting; waiting to smoke us out." It was as if Stellan's mind had melded with Enka's. He could almost hear her counting.

Stellan felt his sister's panic. He looked at Third, who stood rigid with his eyes clamped shut. There had been terrible times when Third had found himself in the bitter landscape of his mother's mind. But now it was as like something had entered him, inhabited him. A voice emanated from the tiny cub, but not his own.

"Follow me!" The words came from Third's mouth, but in a deeper voice that did not belong to him.

"Skagen?" Jytte blurted. It was exactly the voice of the snow leopard.

"Spirit guide," Third muttered in his own voice, and began trotting down the winding passage of the clear air. The two cubs followed. The passage wound deep beneath the ground and then started to climb up through a tangle of roots. The cubs at last emerged into what might have been, at one time, a den. And then not far from them they saw the backs of six bears gathered at the mouth of Skagen's cave. A voice snarled, "It's been forty-five minutes, thirty-seven seconds, and ten milliseconds. Stop the smoking. Let the air clear. We shall enter and find them."

The three cubs watched as the Roguers made preparations to enter the cave. From a few holes dug in the ground they took red-hot coals and enclosed them in two metal boxes, which they put aside. The smoke immediately lessened. Then two bears with the longest claws the cubs had ever seen entered the cave. They were followed by two bears carrying nets, the same kind that had been flung at the cubs on the ice spines. As they disappeared into the cave, Jytte started to rise up and tipped her head in the opposite direction. Stellan shook his head.

"What?" Jytte whispered.

"We can't just run away. We need to make sure they don't catch up with us."

"How?" Third asked. "We're so little. They're gigantic, and those claws!"

"And I swear some had two sets of fangs," Jytte said.

"Fire," Stellan replied evenly.

Jytte blinked at her brother. She had never seen him like this. He seemed confident, unworried, not a shadow of a second thought, and completely resolute. But she felt her insides roiling with fear. The bears' claws were so long it would be easy for them to reach out and snag any of them. The claws were an evil and ingenious weapon that made these deadly bears even deadlier.

They worked quickly. The bears had cleared away most of the junk and debris that had camouflaged the entrance to the cave. The cubs now gathered as much dried brush as they could and began piling it in a big mound at the opening. Then they dumped the coals from the boxes. The brush ignited quickly. The wind suddenly strengthened, and it was as if the cave devoured the flames.

"Won't they find the tunnel that leads out as we did?" Third asked.

"Yes, but it's going to take them a long time!" Jytte said. There was still one box of coals left. She ran and grabbed the box, then headed for the den from which the cubs had emerged a few moments before.

"Shove in those branches with the dried leaves, Stellan!" Third joined him.

"Now!" Stellan said.

Jytte tossed the coals on the leaves, and they ignited.

"They're trapped!" Third exclaimed.

Within seconds it seemed as if the entire gilly forest was wrapped in flames. But the cubs found their way through the conflagration to the sea that beckoned. But in their wake they heard the thunderous rampage of the furious bears and their roars as they ran from the fire.

"And now" — Stellan turned to Jytte and Third — "we must find Skagen." It was not long before they picked up the tracks of the Roguer bears. They had come from Oddsvall, exactly where Skagen had gone. Each cub was in its own mind desperately trying to entertain hope that Skagen had somehow escaped the marauding Roguers. But all hope was extinguished as Jytte tipped her head up and shrieked.

"Look!" Her voice scratched the sky as she pointed to the scavenging birds. The cubs broke into a gallop.

"Hiiiiiyaaaa!" they roared, flailing their arms wildly at four vultures who were on the ground, two more just landed. The cubs rushed the birds, and there in front of them lay the broken body of Skagen. "No! No!" they cried.

The snow leopard's eyes were rolled back in his head. His side was rent with gaping holes where the vultures had torn at the flesh. The crack echoed again in Third's head.

"They broke his spine. Look!" Third said. "Claw marks. Claw marks of bears."

They walked slowly around the snow leopard. The vultures' work had hardly begun, but the marks of bears were all over the body.

"What are we to do?" Third looked at his friends. Huge, glistening tears rolled down his face. "What are we to do?" He was exhausted. Exhausted from his terrible dreams. Exhausted from his second sight. So tired he could not think of what to do next.

Jytte walked up to Third. She put her arm around his shoulders. "Skagen was a creature of the mountains, but he always sought the sea of Nunquivik," she said. "Let's take him to the sea. The inlet is still open. That's what we should do." *Of course*, Third thought, for despite his second sight, he often did not know what to do in the moment. And at that moment it was as if the entire world had skidded out from beneath his feet. He was staggering with grief and doubt and terror.

"Come along, Third. We'll do this together," Jytte said, and gave his shoulder a squeeze.

Epilogue

The three cubs dragged the body past Syvert Hansen's store, down the path that led into the gilly town of Oddsvall, past the huge whale skulls looming in the mist on the beach to the edge where the cubs had first scrambled out of the inlet. In the inlet, a large, glistening ice floe was floating by. So the three cubs swam toward the floe, towing Skagen's body, and pulled him onto it. They floated with him for a while, and then the cubs began to sing the song of the Schrynn Gar winds that Skagen had taught them.

"Oh, the Scrhynn Gar winds are a restless wind
A restless wind they long to wander
Cross the plains and beyond the Grynn
To the land of ice to their wayward kin

To their wayward kin

That's the way of the Schrynn Gar winds."

A sudden breeze blew out of the east; a shadow spread across the floe and with one leap began to walk up into the sky, which was sprinkled with stars. It turned just once and, raising a paw, pointed to the Fighting Bear constellation that was rising in the east and striding toward the west.

The last of the lavender light of the twiliqglow had dissolved, but then there was a mute shudder in the sky as a banner of green unfurled. The three cubs slid off the ice floe and into the black water of the Oddsvall inlet and began to swim.

"Look," Jytte said. "There they are!" She rolled onto her back and floated, looking at the sky.

"Who?" asked Third.

"Us," Stellan said softly. "The two stars in the Great Bear constellation that wander. Our stars — Jytte and Stellan. We've come unstuck again and are skipping ahead of Mum."

By now the sky was flickering with the dancing colors of the ahalikki. Third stopped swimming and was treading water.

"Jytte, Stellan, did you ever dance on an ice floe under the ahalikki with your mum?"

"Yes!" they both said.

"But, Third, how did you know about the dancing? Surely Taaka never danced with you," Stellan asked.

"Never, but I dreamed it."

"It was so long ago that we danced with our mum," Jytte whispered into the night, "that it feels like a dream now to me."

"Oh no!" Third said. "It was real. Besides, to dream is to live." Third paused and then turned to the cubs. "I know what you dream of, what you seek. And together, we'll find it."

He needed no answer. Nor did Jytte and Stellan need to speak. The cubs looked into one another's eyes and felt The Belong. So the three bears swam on toward the bear kingdoms of Ga'Hoole to find the Den of Forever Frost, find their father and hope for their mother, break a clock, and save their own kind.